The Adventures of Commander Didlittle and the Lost Battalion

By Callum James Macgregor

Order this book online at www.trafford.com
or email orders@trafford.com

Most Trafford titles are also available at major online book retailers.

Editing by Amelia Gilliland
Cover and interior illustrations by Valda Oishi
Text design by Amelia Gilliland

Printed in Victoria, BC, Canada.

ISBN: 978-1-4269-0223-9 (sc)
ISBN: 978-1-4269-0224-6 (dj)
ISBN: 978-1-4269-0225-3 (e-book)

*Our mission is to efficiently provide the world's finest, most comprehensive
book publishing service, enabling every author to experience success.
To find out how to publish your book, your way, and have it available
worldwide, visit us online at www.trafford.com*

Trafford rev. 11/13/2009

www.trafford.com

North America & international
toll-free: 1 888 232 4444 (USA & Canada)
phone: 250 383 6864 ♦ fax: 812 355 4082

Dedicated to Gramma, with love

KUMQUAT ISLAND

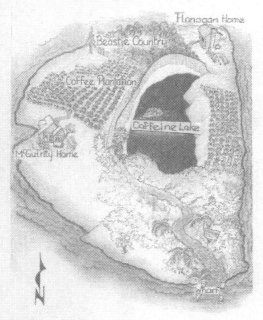

The Military Office of Ordinance
Government Official Office

Under the direction of –
General Higginbottom ,
requisitions – Commander
Didlittle, to head up the rescue
mission of the Flanagan family
who are held captive on Kumquat
Island.

By Order Of

The British Military Command,
The House of Commons,
Her Royal Highness
Queen of England,
and All Who Care.

CHAPTER 1
Summons to Headquarters

General Higginbottom hung up the phone and said to his assistant, "We've got an impossible situation on our hands on Kumquat Island. Get me Didlittle on the phone right away!"

"Sir, I have Didlittle on the phone," said the assistant.

"Hello, Didlittle? I want you here right away!"

"All right, General. This sounds urgent. What's the matter?"

"No questions, Didlittle. Just get to London headquarters immediately."

"Yes, sir. I'm on my way!"

After hanging up the phone, he turned to his aide de camp and said, "Hawksbury, the General has urgently ordered me to London. We're out the door. I'll drive!"

Commander Didlittle and Hawksbury rushed out to their car and zoomed off to the train station. On arrival, Didlittle jumped out and started running to catch a moving train just leaving the station.

"Wait, Commander," yelled Hawksbury.

"Not now, Hawksbury. Can't you see I've got to catch this train before it gets away?"

Didlittle just managed to jump onto the train before it got away from him.

"But, Commander," yelled Hawksbury.

But by now Didlittle and the train had travelled out of earshot and disappeared out of sight.

Commander Didlittle gathered his composure, brushed back his hair, and strutted into the dining car. He sat at an empty table and ordered bangers, mash, and eggs. When the food arrived, he said to the waiter, "I'll need this big breakfast because I've been ordered down to London by General Higginbottom of MOOGOO, who will be sending me and my battalion off to some exotic land to do good deeds for Queen and Country."

The waiter gave Didlittle a stunned look and shook his head.

"Don't shake your head at me, young man. Don't you know who I am? I am Commander Didlittle of the Lost Battalion, and I am a very important man. I travel all over the world doing highly dangerous work for the British military...and the Queen, of course. Don't you shake your head, I am a world traveller, and I can find my way around any part of the world. In fact, I think it can be said that I am one of the most experienced and smartest travellers in the world. Why, just last year we were in India, and if it wasn't for the Bengal tigers, we wouldn't have gotten lost. But that doesn't distract from the fact that I am Commander Didlittle, and I am one of the smartest travellers in the world."

The waiter was waiting for Didlittle to take a breath, and when he finally did, the waiter said, "But, sir, this train isn't going to London."

"It's not? Then where is it going?"

"To Scotland, sir."

"What? Pull the emergency cord! I must get off this train at once."

After the train stopped, Commander Didlittle got off with his bangers, mash, and eggs wrapped in a newspaper. A few minutes later, sitting on the roadside and eating, Didlittle was approached by a local chap who asked, "Where are you going?"

"I'm going to London. Can you help me?"

"Well, I've only got a Mercedes…"

"A Mercedes, that's perfect! How about giving me a ride to London? This is an emergency!"

"Okay."

The two walked down the road to the nearest farmhouse. A few moments later, Didlittle and the chap appeared on the street riding on an old hay wagon.

"You didn't tell it was a Mercedes hay wagon."

"You didn't ask," the man said.

"How long will it take for the hay wagon to get to London?"

"Oh, about five days or so."

"That will never do. I am on urgent MOOGOO business and must be in London as soon as possible."

"Well, if I don't spare the horses, I can get you there in four days."

Commander Didlittle sat quietly alongside the farmer in an intense state of frustration and thought about what his transportation alternatives were, aside from the hay wagon. Then he saw a

Porsche coming up the road, and quick as a flash, Didlittle pulled out his flare gun and fired a distress signal into the air. The red flair lit up the sky, and the Porsche came to a stop alongside the hay wagon. Didlittle jumped down and marched with authority up to the driver of the Porsche.

"I am Commander Didlittle, and I have urgent business at MOOGOO Headquarters in London. I need you to take me there immediately!"

The driver, obviously very impressed with Didlittle's authoritative military manner, said, "Yes, of course."

Four hours later, the Porsche pulled up in front of MOOGOO Headquarters.

CHAPTER 2
The Mission

"What took you so long, Didlittle?"

"Well, sir, I started for London and then I ended up going to Scotland and then I caught a Mercedes but that turned out to be a hay wagon and then..."

"Enough! I don't want to hear anymore. Step over to the map. I want to show you your next impossible, no, challenging mission. As you know, Didlittle, I only send you out on the challenging assignments because somehow you always come back, even though we're sure you and your Lost Battalion don't have a chance. Well, never mind. Let's get on with it, shall we?"

"Study the map carefully, Didlittle. What do you see?"

"I see a big coffee cup stain in the middle of the map."

"Very good, and that's where you're going: off the coast of Costa Rica, where the finest coffee is grown."

"But, sir, Costa Rica is a beautiful and peaceful country. Why would we need to go there?"

"Because our agent there has reported that the Kumquat Island Coffee Company plantation has been taken over by a rebel group who we've code-named the Teeny Weenie Meanies. They're small but they pack a powerful punch, and we think they're holding the owner's family, the Flanagans, as hostages. I want you and your battalion to go in and rescue them. Get your battalion out to the airport for an early morning take off, with full parachute gear, of course."

CHAPTER 3
The Parachute Drop

The next morning, the Lost Battalion climbed aboard airplanes equipped for a parachute drop somewhere near Costa Rica.

When the planes were safely in the air, Commander Didlittle said to Hawksbury, "Why didn't you tell me that train was going to Scotland?"

"I tried, sir, but you were too far away when I yelled."

"Very well, Hawk. Let's get some shuteye."

"But, sir, shouldn't we study the map to be sure we know the exact location of the drop zone?"

"Don't worry, Hawk. You don't know the tricks of long-distance travel. All we have to do is calculate the hours needed to get there, set our watches, and jump when the travel time is up. I've already done the calculation, and we need to be in the air for nine hours. I told the pilot to wake us in time so that we can be ready to jump. So relax and get some sleep."

Didlittle leaned back on the stiff paratrooper bench, dropped his chin to his chest, and promptly went to sleep, signalled by a slight snore.

Hawksbury sat nervously looking at Didlittle and worried about the dangers that lay ahead. After a few moments, he could hear the snoring of the rest of the troops, who seemed to fall asleep as soon as they heard Didlittle snoring, and he then fell into a fitful sleep himself.

"Now hear this. This is the Pilot speaking, Commander Didlittle. We're almost at the nine-hour mark. Prepare the battalion for the parachute drop."

"All right, men. It's time to jump."

"But Commander, I thought you said we were landing in a coffee plantation," said Hawk.

"That's right, we are."

"But Commander, there's only ocean below us."

"Not to worry, it's only a mirage. The eyes play tricks on you in the tropics. Now get ready to jump."

"But Commander..."

"No more buts, Hawksbury. Now away you go, out of the plane, like a good lad."

A few moments later, all six hundred men of the Lost Battalion were floating in parachutes in the clear blue sky.

"Commander, I think we're going to land in the ocean."

"I told you, it's just a mirage, Hawksbury."

"But, sir, I can see whitecaps and seagulls."

"Oh, Hawksbury, you're such a worrywart," said Didlittle, just as he splashed into the ocean.

"YEEGADS, what is this!"

"It's the ocean, sir," said Hawksbury.

"Very well then, we'll carry on as planned."

"But, sir, how can we carry on as planned when we're in the water?"

"Don't argue with me, Hawksbury. We'll proceed directly to find the plantation."

"Sir, how can we proceed to find the plantation when we can't even find land?"

"Now that's a good point, Hawksbury, a very good point."

At that point the whole battalion was floating in the ocean waiting for orders from their Commander.

CHAPTER 4
Welcome Aboard

While bobbing up and down in the rolling sea, Commander Didlittle thought about what his next move should be. He was thankful that he had insisted all of his men put on a life jacket before they jumped from the plane.

Just then, Hawksbury yelled out, "Look, Commander Didlittle, there's a boat on the horizon!"

Didlittle whipped out his rusty but trusty telescope and saw a tug pulling a barge. Without a moment's hesitation, he fired off three signal flares to signify S.O.S. (save our souls). The flares gave off a bright red glow in the sky.

Didlittle and all the troops watched anxiously as the tug continued on the horizon without any change in its course. Then the tug slowly turned and started heading towards them.

The large ocean-going tug, with its high rubber-belted bow, steamed slowly as it neared the floating troops and finally came to a full stop. The bright red upper cabin contrasted with the black hull was a most welcome sight to Didlittle and his troops.

After a few minutes, Didlittle and Hawksbury were taken aboard the tug. They were led to the upper cabin where, as they stepped over the raised sill of the wheelhouse, they saw a tall, gaunt officer with a black beard holding the helm.

"Welcome aboard! I'm Captain Quag. I'm sure you have quite a story to tell."

Didlittle replied, "Thank you for rescuing us, Captain. I am Commander Didlittle, and I am traveling on urgent MOOGOO business. Our destination is Kumquat Island. Do you also have room on board this ship for the six hundred men of the Lost Battalion?"

"Well, Commander, you are a very lucky man for two reasons. First of all, this tug is the Kumquat Queen, and we are heading to Kumquat Island. Second of all, our empty barge has lots of room for your troops. Now you two go below and get dried off, and we'll get your men pulled up onto the barge."

Within an hour, all of the men of the Lost Battalion had been brought safely aboard the barge, and the tug was once again underway.

"So, you are headed for Kumquat Island. What takes you there?" asked Didlittle.

"We're going there to pick up a barge-load of coffee beans."

"Really? Do you go there often?"

"Yeah, about once a month. It's a beautiful island, but right now it's a dangerous place. You see, the owners, the Flanagan family, have been taken hostage."

"For how long?" asked Didlittle.

"About two months."

"Why doesn't somebody try to rescue them?"

"Oh, they've tried, but every rescue squad that's gone in has never been heard from again."

"What's happened to them?"

"Don't know. They just seem to have disappeared."

"Are these rebels asking a high ransom?"

"Not exactly."

"What do you mean?"

"Well, they're not exactly rebels and it isn't a ransom they're after."

"Well, what do they want then?"

Captain Quag reached into a small barrel, pulled out a dried hunk of squid with long tentacles hanging down, and said, "Do you care for a chew of squiggly squid?"

Didlittle and Hawksbury recoiled at the thought of chewing something so awful looking and foul smelling.

"No, thank you," they said in unison.

The captain took a big bite of the squid and started to chew with delight. After wiping away some residue from his beard, he continued with his answer.

"First of all, the rebels, as you call them, are the McGuinty family. The family is headed up by the father, Squinty McGuinty. They are holding the Flanagans captive until they agree to let their beautiful daughter, Monica, marry Tobius McGuinty, their son."

"Is Tobius a handsome chap?"

"I would say so."

"Is he a bad person?"

"No."

"Is he a man of means?"

"Oh, yes. His family owns half of the Kumquat Coffee Company, he's a plantation foreman, he's a world-class water skier, and he builds the most beautiful speed boats."

"So why won't the Flanagans let him marry their daughter, Monica?"

"He's only six inches tall."

"Oh my, that is a problem. What about the rest of the McGuinty family?"

"All the same: six inches tall."

"Thank you, captain, for a summary of the situation at the Kumquat Island Coffee plantation. Let me introduce myself properly. I am Commander Didlittle, and this is my aide de camp, Hawksbury. We have been dispatched by MOOGOO."

Didlittle held back a moment, anticipating an acknowledgement of respect. Silence.

The captain asked, "Do you mean Moo Goo Guy Pan? I like that dish, especially with a good helping of squid."

Didlittle stiffened up to a full attention posture and loudly responded, "No, I do not mean Moo Goo Guy Pan. I mean the world famous British Military Intelligence Unit that fights crime, corruption, and nastiness all around the world."

"Oh, you mean MOO GOO! But of course, the Military Office of Ordinance, Government Official Office. Why didn't you tell me? And you are the famous Commander Didlittle. And the troops, they are your Lost Battalion. By the way, how did you manage to get lost in India?"

"Never mind that for now. We have been assigned to rescue the Flanagans, and we could use your assistance."

"Of course, Commander Didlittle. We'll help in any way we can. May I ask one question?"

"What would you like to know?"

"How did you and your six hundred men end up floating around in the Pacific Ocean?"

"That, my good sir, is a military secret!"

"Oh, yes, of course. Are you sure you don't want a bite of this squiggly squid?"

"No, thank you. But you could help by dropping me and my men off in an isolated cove on Kumquat Island."

"Of course. I know the perfect spot! It's an unused wharf where no one will see you arrive."

"Perfect. How long until we arrive?"

"Eight hours."

"Great. Wake me when we arrive."

Didlittle and Hawksbury retired to rest in the officers' quarters selected for them by the captain.

"What are you planning to do, sir?" asked Hawksbury.

"Since I'm lying horizontal on this bunk with a pillow under my head, isn't it obvious that I'm planning to sleep?"

"But, sir, we'll soon be landing on Kumquat Island. Every rescue squad that's gone in before has disappeared, and we don't have a plan of action!"

"Oh, Hawk, don't be so melodramatic. I have a plan. It just hatched into my head."

"And what is that, sir?"

"When we meet these pesky little rebels, we'll just say that they are to surrender or we'll squash them like bugs."

"But, sir, don't you think that the previous rescue squads might have thought of that approach?"

"Hawk, as you well know, I got to where I am today because I am a military genius. Don't make the mistake of thinking that other officers could be thinking what I'm thinking because I'm thinking all the time. Did you ever think of that?"

"No, sir. I mean, yes, sir. I mean, whatever you say, sir."

"Very good, Hawk. Now run along, and wake me when we get to Kumquat Island."

CHAPTER 5
The Warning

The sun was just about to set as the tug and barge off-loaded Commander Didlittle and the Lost Battalion at the old deserted wharf. The wharf, built completely out of wood timber, was bleached to a blonde hue by the tropical sun. Although the planks creaked as Didlittle marched his men down the wharf, it was obviously still a very sturdy structure.

Didlittle led the troops off the wharf and up an old gravel road, which snaked its way through a wilderness of tropical vegetation in many shapes and sizes. A bull frog croaking, wild bird calls, and loud cricket chatter told them there was lots of animal and insect life in the jungle around them.

After a few minutes marching, Hawksbury yelled, "Look at the sign hanging in the tree!"

Sure enough, hanging high enough in the trees so that all could see was a large sign that read:

WARNING! THIS ISLAND IS NOW OCCUPIED
AND ALL TRESPASSERS WILL BE PUNISHED.
RETURN TO THE WHARF AND EXIT THIS
ISLAND IMMEDIATELY!

"What should we do, Commander Didlittle?" asked Hawksbury.

Didlittle replied, "Ignore the sign and keep the troops moving."

The troop marched farther into the jungle. Suddenly, a loud voice boomed out, "You never heed a warning, do you, Didlittle?"

"Who is that, and what's your intention, and where are you?" asked Didlittle.

"Didlittle, I ask the questions. That is, if there's any need for them. This is your last warning. Turn your troops around and get off this island, and I mean now. I repeat, this is your last warning."

A long silence followed.

"What do we do now, Commander?" asked Hawksbury.

"We will keep marching onward. That threat means nothing."

The troops marched onward and upward through the jungle on the old plantation road. They were very impressed with the wide array of animals and birds in the trees. There were numerous monkeys that just hung on the limbs and watched as the battalion passed by. And there were beautiful parrots with bright blue, green, yellow, and red plumage that cawed away as if to alert the island that there were visitors. And everywhere there were the friendly and flighty hummingbirds buzzing from flower to flower.

Eventually, they came into a clearing that revealed a lush valley leading down towards a large lake. The lake extended up the valley as far as the eye could see. There wasn't a ripple on its surface so it reflected the late sun like a mirror, which gave it a strange and spooky appearance.

"We'll march down to the lake and set up camp at its edge," said Didlittle.

With these instructions, Hawksbury passed the command on to the troops.

As the troops approached the dark-coloured lake, the loud voice boomed out at them again. "You just won't take "Not Welcome" for an answer, will you, Didlittle? For the last time, I command you to return to the wharf immediately and leave this island."

"Look, Squinty Twinty Winty Mcquinty, or whatever your name is, your big booming voice doesn't scare me. I know you're only six inches tall and you're just trying to scare us off by amplifying your voice with a stereo system."

"Oh, very good, Didlittle. Well, you can't say I didn't warn you. Oh, by the way, I'll make you a promise."

"Yes, and just what would that promise be?" asked Didlittle.

"That before I'm through with you, you'll treat me with respect and you'll address me as Squinty McGuinty, Esquire."

"Oh, get real! You're only six inches tall."

"Never mind, you've been warned."

CHAPTER 6
The Water Show

"What do we do now, Commander?" Hawksbury asked with trepidation.

"Set up the tents on that white sand beach near the lake, and get the cook to whip us up some chow. The troops will be hungry by now."

After dinner, Didlittle and the troops bunked down in their tents for a good sleep after the long day's journey.

"Lights out," yelled Hawksbury, as is his nightly duty.

Soon the camp was in darkness, and everybody was just dozing off to sleep, when suddenly the loud voice boomed out, "So you don't think my six-inch folk are a match for the famous Commander Didlittle and his troops? Well, just watch us put you all into Caffeine Lake, which you'll find to be full of a lukewarm coffee tar. McGuintys, begin the tickle attack!"

As soon as the command had been given, the troops started rolling around in their sleeping bags and scratching furiously. Driven into a frenzy, the soldiers rushed into Caffeine Lake for relief. Eventually the entire troop, including Didlittle and Hawksbury, were in the lake.

"Welcome to Caffeine Lake, Commander Didlittle. You and your troops are now totally immersed in coffee tar. This liquid has such a high specific gravity that you will be unable to resist any pressure placed upon you."

By now, total darkness had descended upon the valley and with the dark-coloured coffee-tar lake surrounding them, Didlittle and the troops couldn't see anything but blackness.

The bad thing about the dark, murky coffee tar they stood in was that they could hardly move their limbs. But the good thing was that it was restful, slightly warm, and quite comfortable. Because of the thickness of the black coffee-tar liquid of the lake, the troops could lean back and float without any effort.

After a short while, the effortless relaxation of floating in the thick liquid seemed to put the entire troop into a trance. As they floated peacefully on their backs in a weird stupor, a light cord was lassoed around each soldier and they were silently pulled across the lake.

Commander Didlittle blinked his eyes open to face a bright morning sun shining on the lake and the verdant valley surrounding them. With the bright daylight, he was initially bewildered, but then he remembered that he was totally immersed in the coffee tar of Caffeine Lake. By now, the entire troop was awake.

A loud voice said, "Good Morning, Didlittle. It looks like you and your troops had a good sleep. You soldiers are fortunate that you arrived at Caffeine Lake when you did because today we are holding our annual water-show regatta. Eyes right everybody, and let the show begin!"

Looking to their right, the troops saw an island in the lake. Out from behind the island zoomed a beautiful teakwood speedboat with shiny brass rail trim pulling three water-skiers. As the water-skiers approached the troops, they started doing 360 degree turns, back-flips, and summersaults. And then they started criss-crossing as they did their incredible jumps and turns again.

No sooner had this speedboat passed by when three equally beautiful speedboats appeared pulling five skiers with three standing up on their shoulders. The show continued for over half an hour with the most fantastic water tricks anyone had ever seen.

"And now, soldiers, you will see all the skiers from our show at once."

A loud roaring sound from behind the island preceded the appearance of seven beautiful speedboats pulling twenty-one skiers, who had five levels of skiers standing on top of each other with a single skier on the top holding a sign that read, "The McGuintys will stand tall again someday."

It was only then, with the reference to size, that it dawned on the troops that the skiers were only six inches tall and the speedboats only eighteen inches long.

After a few minutes, a voice boomed out, "Well, how did you like the show?"

Didlittle replied, "I must admit, McGuinty, you do put on one pip of a water show."

"Thank you, Didlittle. You're showing a little more respect. You're not saying that squinty winky stuff, but I shall want you to address me as Squinty McGuinty, Esquire."

"Never!" Didlittle replied.

"Never say never, Commander Didlittle. You don't know what's coming next. Okay, boys, bring the workboats."

CHAPTER 7
Refuge Beach

O ut from behind the island appeared a squadron of tugs making a loud, powerful roaring sound. The tugs came up close to the troops and then slowly turned around. The fact that these tugs were only thirty-six inches long didn't matter. After seeing what the eighteen-inch speedboats could do, these tugs looked big to the troops.

The tugs appeared to hook up to a main tow-line and then the troops realized that they were still all tethered together. With the steady towing pressure of the tugs, the troops started to move in the direction the tugs were pulling.

After several hours of towing, a white, sandy beach came into view. As they moved closer, the troops saw people on the beach. They also saw that the beach was surrounded by a very tall bamboo fence. As they got closer still, Hawksbury said, "This must be the stockade where they are holding all the rescue squads."

"Quite right, Hawk, quite right. Once they release us from these lassos, we'll go ashore and speak to the ranking officer."

A few minutes later, the tugs sounded a shrill whistle and the ropes around each soldier went slack and were pulled away. As Didlittle and Hawksbury led the troops up onto the beach, a big, hefty soldier with a large red handle-bar moustache stepped forward and said, "Welcome to Refuge Beach, Commander. We heard you were coming to rescue us, sir! My name is Sydney Stinkworthy, sir. I was the leading rank on the beach until you arrived. I am a Sergeant Major, sir. I believe in strict military discipline, sir. Is there anything I can do for you, sir?"

"Well, to begin with, Stinkworthy, you can stop saying 'Sir' all the time. You're giving me a headache already."

"Yes, sir. I understand, sir."

"All right, Stinkworthy, you can start by giving me an officer's summary of the situation."

"Yes, sir. Right, sir. Well, as you can see, we have a wide assortment of people here who came to rescue the Flanagans. Obviously we've all failed, but then none of us had the wide experience and military genius of someone as famous as you, sir."

"Quite right, Stinkworthy, quite right."

"Sir, may I say allowing yourselves to be captured so that you would be brought right into Refuge Beach without needing to fight your way in is absolutely brilliant, sir. Absolutely brilliant! I hope you don't mind me saying so, sir."

"No, not at all, Stinkworthy. You're very clever to see that I purposely allowed us to be captured. That was the secret strategy I used. It was so secret that my own troops didn't even know. Isn't that so, Hawk?"

"Yes, sir. I mean, no, sir. I mean, whatever you said sir, is right, sir."

Stinkworthy stepped closer to Didlittle and said in a lowered voice, "What is the plan you've got for our escape. You can tell me. My lips are sealed, sir."

Commander Didlittle stepped back and said, "Stink, I'm surprised to see such audacity from a Sergeant Major. And besides, it's a military secret."

"Sorry, sir. Of course, sir. I understand, sir."

"Good, now I want to talk to the most knowledgeable person in the stockade about Kumquat Island. Who would that be?"

"That would be Doggie MacDonald. He's sitting over there under the palm tree. I'll introduce you to him."

Stinkworthy led Didlittle and Hawksbury over to a most curious-looking individual. He was sitting in the shade of the palm tree with his legs tucked under him and his upper body was resting on his outstretched arms. His long blonde hair and beard gave him a shaggy appearance. As he crouched under the tree's shade with his tongue hanging out, he definitely had a dog-like appearance.

"Good morning, Doggie. I'd like you to meet Commander Didlittle. He is the famous Commander of the Lost Battalion and they've come to rescue us."

"You mean rescue you and all the others here who came to rescue the Flanagans. Don't include me."

"Let's dispense with the formalities, shall we Doggie MacDonald? I understand you're the one with the most knowledge about Kumquat Island. Is that so?" asked Commander Didlittle.

"It had better be, since I've spent nearly my entire life on the island."

"Have you never been off the island?"

"Oh, yes. Once I left to attend college for a while, but that is another story."

"Not now, Doggie MacDonald. I need to know how you got to this island and how you know it so well."

"Well, it all started... " said Doggie MacDonald as he reached into his pocket and pulled out a package of doggie biscuits. "Care for a doggie biscuit? These are pure bone meal with T-bone flavouring. They're delicious."

"No, thank you. Please continue."

"Well, as I understand it, it all started with a cruise ship voyage my parents took me on when I was just a baby. Somehow I fell overboard but nobody noticed because the ship kept sailing right along. Fortunately, my parents had me strapped into a baby carrier that was floatable, and the currents brought me onto the shore of this island. A dog pack came along and found me and took me to their den. My first few years were spent in that den with the dog family that cared for me very well. You probably haven't noticed, but I do have the odd doggie-like characteristic."

"But you didn't spend you whole childhood with the dogs. When did you leave them?"

"One day, I was running with a pack of puppies and we saw a young boy and girl playing on the beach. This was the first time I'd seen a human being and it gave me a funny feeling. You see, my doggie parents never told me I wasn't a dog. I just thought I was an unusual-looking dog. But when I saw these two children, I felt a strong sense of attraction to them. They just seemed so much like, I don't know, like family. Anyway, we ran down to them in a pack and started playing with them. They started throwing sticks for us to retrieve. When I returned the stick to the girl, she gave me a big hug and said to her brother, "This puppy is so adorable, I'm going to take him home. What do you think, Jason?"

"You're always bringing stray animals home, Monica. Don't you think Mom and Dad are getting tired of feeding and caring for them?"

"But Jason, this puppy is so different. He's looks so, I don't know, he looks so human-like. I could almost see him as another brother."

"Oh, Monica, that is so ridiculous. But if you really want to bring him home, I'll agree, if you can get him to come with you voluntarily."

"All right, Jason. That's a deal."

Monica then took out a package of dog biscuits and called me over, "Here, doggie-doggie, here doggie-doggie."

Doggie MacDonald cleared his throat with a load barking cough and continued. "You see, I was raised in a den of wild dogs and survived on the grubs and berries of the wild. I'd never tasted a doggie biscuit before and the aroma emanating from the biscuit in Monica's hand was, to be perfectly frank, irresistible. I ran over and gobbled up the biscuit. Monica picked me up and said, "I have more biscuits at home. Would you like some more?"

"And that was when the most remarkable thing happened. Instead of uttering my usual bow-wow sound of agreement, I said 'Sure.' Well, let me tell you, I don't know who was more surprised, Monica or me. When we arrived home, Monica said to her parents, 'Look at what I got: a dog that talks.'"

Mr. Flanagan took one look at me and brushed my doggie mane aside to inspect my face. He then brushed aside the leaves and branches stuck in my extremities from running wild in the jungle.

After the inspection, Mr. Flanagan said, "You know, Monica, you haven't brought home a stray dog. You've brought home a stray human being."

From that day on, I became part of the Flanagan family, with Monica treating me like her brother. Jason never did figure out where I stood with him and vice-versa."

"Did you go to the mainland to attend college?" asked Didlittle.

"Yes, I did, and I was away for four years."

"What did you study?"

"Doggyology."

"So you've lived on this island for your whole life since being lost at sea, except the four years at college?"

"That's right."

"Then you must know every inch of it."

"That I do."

Didlittle was starting to feel better. It sounded like he had found the person who could give him the intelligence he needed to accomplish a successful rescue of the Flanagan family.

CHAPTER 8
The Impossible Mission Plan

Commander Didlittle continued his questioning. "What exactly is going on at the Kumquat Coffee plantation?"

"Now that is a very good question," said Doggie MacDonald as he pulled out a package from his pocket. "Anyone care for a doggie biscuit?"

"No, no, just go on with your story."

"Okay, first of all, you need to know that the Flanagans and the McGuintys were very close friends. The McGuintys did the planting and harvesting of the coffee beans and the Flanagans made the coffee and ran the business. They were life-long friends and there were plans in place for Tobius McGuinty and Monica Flanagan to be wed this past spring."

"But what about Tobius only being six inches tall? Wasn't that a problem?"

"Well, it is now, but the McGuintys weren't always six inches tall. You see, they were normal-sized people. In fact, the boys were all over six feet tall until late last year. Then one day, poof, they were only six inches tall."

"What caused the sudden shrinkage?" Didlittle asked.

"That's the sixty-four-dollar question. Nobody knows."

"Did the hostage-taking happen after the McGuintys got shrunk?"

"That's right, about a week later," replied Doggie.

"It sounds to me like these two incidents are related," said Didlittle.

"They might be, but nobody knows for sure," replied Doggie.

"Where are the Flanagans being held captive?"

"Well, nobody knows for sure because nobody's been able to get to the Flanagan home on the plantation, but I'd bet that's where they are."

"We must get to the Flanagans and find out exactly what's going on. Can you lead us to the Flanagan home?" asked Didlittle.

"Of course. I lived on the plantation most of my life."

"Good. Now is there a way for us to get out of this stockade?" Didlittle asked.

"Oh sure, that's easy. But that's not the biggest challenge to getting to the Flanagan home," said Doggie.

"What do you mean?"

"Okay, first of all, the twenty-foot bamboo stockade fence surrounding this beach is only sunk two feet into the ground. With my doggie upbringing, I can dig a hole under the fence in five minutes with my paws, er...hands, I mean."

"Then why haven't you escaped?" asked Didlittle.

"Because the McGuintys patrol the fence-line in the daytime. And at nighttime when the McGuintys are asleep, the area outside the bamboo fence is where the Beastie Boars wander looking for food."

"Beastie Boars? I've never heard of them," said Didlittle.

"Oh, they are a nasty piece of business, Commander," piped in Stinkworthy.

"Tell me, Stinkworthy, how would you know about the Beastie Boars?" Didlittle asked.

"Well, sir, when my rescue squadron and I first landed on the island, we managed to get inland undetected by the McGuintys, and at nightfall we set up a tent camp not far from here. Just as we were going to sleep, we heard a snorting sound that seemed to get louder and louder. We sprung out of our sleeping bags and shone a flashlight towards the snorting sounds, and there, not twenty feet from us, was a pack of these Beastie Boars. Oh, they were a mean looking sight. They were all black with long tusks and brilliant green eyes that seemed to shine out at you like lasers."

"This was a tight situation, as we only had two rifles. The rest of our equipment had been stashed in a waterproof locker that was right were the Beasties stood. Not only that, but also the two rifles we had were not loaded. Fortunately, I and my men had experience in India with Bengal tigers, and we knew that if we ran for it, these Beasties would run us down and we'd be done for."

"I ordered my riflemen to take aim at the lead Beastie as if the guns were loaded. Our experience with Bengals told us that the pack won't attack until the leader does. We also knew that the lead Beastie would be the smartest and with two guns aimed at him, he'd hesitate leading the charge. After waiting a minute to make sure everybody, especially the lead Beastie, understood the situation, I ordered my squad to commence retreating very slowly in tight military formation down the road. As we retreated, the Beasties followed closely, looking for an opportunity to attack. My riflemen maintained a bead on the lead Beastie, and we continued to back down the road until we came upon this stockade. The light and noise of the prisoners inside scared off the Beasties, but we got captured the next morning by the McGuintys. But better the Mc-Guintys than the Beasties. As I said before, they are a nasty piece of business."

"So, once we leave the stockade, we'll likely have to deal with the Beasties. Is that all?" asked Didlittle.

"Well, yes, but doesn't that make this mission impossible?" asked Doggie.

"Of course it does, and that's why I'm here: To lead us on an impossible mission. That's my specialty."

"But, sir, didn't I hear that you lost all your rifles when you were captured?" asked Stinkworthy.

"It's true that they confiscated all our rifles, but they didn't take away our special supplies," replied Didlittle.

"What do you mean?" asked Stinkworthy.

"Come, come, my dear Sergeant, surely you know that one of the O's in MOOGOO stands for Ordinance, which stands for special weapons?"

"Oh, my goodness. You mean you still have all your special weapons of destruction? That's fantastic. Commander, you are a genius!"

"Yes, yes, I've often been told that, but it's just a matter of me having so much experience and knowledge in the field of combat, and, of course, I have a wonderful ability to expect the unexpected. But enough about me, it's time for action."

"Hawksbury, muster up Platoon G and have them report to me on the double," Didlittle commanded.

"Are you sure, sir? I mean, don't you remember that you...?" said Hawksbury.

"Hawk, didn't you just hear me say that we'd talked enough about my military expertise and that now was the time for action? Did you hear me say that?" demanded Didlittle.

"Yes, sir," Hawksbury replied.

"And what, I say, what did I just command you to do?"

"To muster up Platoon G, sir."

"Good, then get to it and on the double!" commanded Didlittle. And Hawksbury was off and running.

"All right, Doggie, show me how well you've been canine trained. Dig us a hole under this fence that will let us out as soon as possible."

CHAPTER 9
Escape from Refuge Beach

Doggie dug into his pocket, took out one more doggie biscuit, munched into it with relish, and said, "This is just to get me back into the mood." Then he crouched down on all fours, ran over to the bamboo fence, and started sniffing along the ground.

"What on earth is he doing?" wondered Didlittle aloud.

"He's looking for a weak spot in the fence-line, I think. Oh, he's found a spot he likes. Good grief, look at how fast he can dig," said Stinkworthy with awe.

Within a few minutes, Doggie had dug an escape tunnel under the fence.

"You should be able to move your Platoon through that without any trouble, Commander," said Doggie with a degree of pride.

"Well done, Doggie. In the name of the Queen and with the authority delegated to me by General Higginbottom of MOOGOO, I am requisitioning you to the battalion and bestowing upon you the temporary title of Royal Pathfinder for the duration of this mission," announced Didlittle.

"Really? Oh, ruff ruff, bow wow, bow wow. Excuse me, but I tend to bark when I get excited. You know, I wasn't planning on going with you on this mission, but now that you've offered me the title of Royal Pathfinder, I feel honoured to be with you in the service of the Queen and MOOGOO. Count me in."

"That's the spirit, Doggie. Now where are Hawksbury and Platoon G?"

No sooner had Didlittle spoke when Hawk approached with Platoon G behind him.

"All right, men, I know Hawksbury has briefed you and you know that you're setting out on an impossible and highly dangerous mission with me. Anyone who wishes to back out can do so now, no questions asked."

In unison, the whole platoon said, "Oh, no, Commander, we have no idea what your plan is but you've always managed to get us all in the most dangerous and impossible situations and you always get us out. We have become famous as the Lost Battalion because of you, so lead on, Commander Didlittle!"

"That's the spirit, men. Now, I see you have your special weapons in their canvas bags with you. It looks like we're ready to go. Good, then let's get through this escape tunnel and we'll regroup on the outside of the bamboo fence."

Turning to his troops, Commander Didlittle roared out the battle cry of the Lost Battalion, "Tally Ho!" and crawled down through the tunnel to the outside.

A few minutes later, the last soldier came through the tunnel and rushed up to stand at attention before Didlittle, flanked by Stinkworthy and Hawk, with Doggie at the back.

"All right, men, let's have a look at the special weapons we have in those canvas bags," said Didlittle.

All the soldiers looked at each other with quizzical expressions on their faces and began to remove the canvas covers.

First to appear was a skinny black clarinet, then a couple of trumpets, then came the trombones, then bassos and tubas and the big bass drum.

In a few short moments, there was the full instrumentation of the Battalion's marching band.

Stinkworthy was thunderstruck by what he saw. "Commander, what on earth do we have here?"

"That's right, Hawk, what do we have here? These are supposed to be the grenadiers of the G platoon with special weapons of destruction!" Didlittle shouted.

"Well, sir, I tried to remind you that you decided to change the grenadiers of G platoon with the musicians of M Platoon so that spies wouldn't know where to find our weapons of destruction. The grenadiers of G platoon are now in M Platoon and the musicians of M Platoon are now in G Platoon. So when you called for G platoon, you were calling for the musicians."

"Ah, yes. Quite right, quite right, and so I did, and so I did," replied Didlittle, thinking of what his next words should be. After a pause, he ordered the men to mount up their instruments.

"With respect, sir, what, may I ask, are you doing?" asked Stinkworthy.

"Why, we're mustering up to start our march into the jungle and onto the Flanagan plantation," replied Didlittle.

"But how can we go out into that jungle at night without weapons to protect us from the Beasties? It's suicide!"

"Oh, piffle. You are so melodramatic, Stinkworthy. My plans always work. What do you say, men?" yelled Didlittle.

The troops of Platoon G came to attention and began to sing in perfect harmony:

"Oh, how we love our Commander,
and love him we truly, truly dooooo.
When we're really in a stew,
who's the one who follows through?
That, of course, is our Commander.

Oh, how we love our Commander,
and love him we truly, truly dooooo.
He may be the one that gets us lost,
but who's the one who saves us at any cost?
That, of course, is our Commander."

"Okay, that's enough for now men, stand easy," commanded Didlittle as he turned to Stinkworthy. "You'll be interested to know that there are another forty-eight verses to that song that show how much my troops admire me and my military genius. Any other comments, Stinkworthy?"

"No, sir!"

"Now, just when are we likely to encounter these so-called Beastie Boars, Stinkworthy?"

"Not likely to see anything until we get up into the high valley, which is where they hunt for their food. But, no matter, we'll hear their snorting when they're close, Commander. Sir, may I ask a personal question?"

"What's that, Stinkworthy?"

"If we don't have any guns, how will we get through the Beastie Boar country without being wiped out by the Beasties?"

"Good question, Stinkworthy, but no need to answer right now. It's a military secret."

CHAPTER 10
The Military Secret

Commander Didlittle led Platoon G into the dreaded jungle night, with Stinkworthy, Hawksbury, and Doggie following nervously. Nobody but Didlittle seemed to have any idea what the next manoeuvre would be.

As they proceeded up the jungle road, it got darker and darker and scarier and scarier. Even the hard-nosed Sergeant-Major Stinkworthy was starting to shudder. Didlittle seemed to be the only one not afraid of the dark and dangerous situation.

Eventually, the sound of birdcalls quieted and then the slow, low sound of snorting could be heard by all in the troop.

"That's the Beastie Boars off in the distance," said Stinkworthy.

"How far away would you say they are, Stink?" asked Didlittle.

"I would estimate them to be approximately twenty-five to thirty minutes away at the rate we are marching."

"Good, then we'll stop for a brief rest in fifteen minutes, and I'll describe my plan to everyone."

Fifteen minutes later, the sound of the snorting was getting quite loud, and more and more pairs of laser-like green eyes appeared all around them. By this time, Stinkworthy and Hawksbury were certain that they were all done for as the green-eyed Beasties moved in on them.

By now, the Beasties had closed in on the troop. They made menacing moves at them and bared their fangs. White, foamy saliva oozed from their mouths at the prospect of dining on the flesh of these foolish humans. Just when it looked like the Beasties were about to attack, Commander Didlittle lifted his baton and announced, "We'll now start with that famous tune, 'What Shall We Do with a Drunken Sailor.'"

The band began to play on the commencing sound of the cymbals clashing and the troop kept right on marching.

"I now want to hear some singing from all who are not playing their instruments and that includes you two, Stink and Hawk. I'll lead."

> "Oh, Oh, Oh, what do you do with a drunken sailor,
> what do you do with a drunken sailor,
> what do you do with a drunken sailor,
> early in the morning.
>
> Way, hey, and up she rises,
> way, hey, and up she rises,
> way, hey, and up she rises,
> early in the morning."

By now, with the full band playing and the rest singing, every Beastie on the island was running over to see the parade. All the while, the Beasties kept snorting, baring their sharp, scary fangs, and staring with their ominous-looking, laser-like, green eyes.

Yet they stepped aside when Didlittle marched towards them and let the marching troops pass by. It seemed they were itching to attack the troop and make a meal of them, but they held back. Why did they hold back? Did they like the sound of the band and the singing? Or were they just confused by the absurdity of a

Commander leading his troops un-armed through their territory at night? No one had ever done that before and maybe that's what confused them.

Whatever the answer, Didlittle and the troop passed out of the Beastie country, and before long they marched right up to the front door of the Flanagan's home.

With a strong rap-rap on the door, Didlittle let the household know that he'd arrived.

CHAPTER 11
Meeting the Flanagans

The front door swung open. "You must be Commander Didlittle! Welcome. I am Matt Flanagan, head of the Flanagan family and plantation. Do come in."

"Thank you, don't mind if I do. Just one moment please," said Didlittle as he turned to his men. "Well done, men. Stand down and take a load off your feet. Hawk, Doggie, come with me. Stinkworthy, you stay outside and keep an eye on the men."

"Ah, yes sir, but sir, don't you think I could be more help inside with you, sir?" asked Stinkworthy with an unexpectedly resistive tone.

"No, I don't, Stink. I think you'll be plenty helpful staying out here with the men."

"But sir, I could be helpful with my experience at Refuge Beach and my strict military strategic thinking. Just like you, sir. Wouldn't you think I could help you with developing a strategic plan, sir?" asked Stinkworthy as he changed from a resistive to a pleading tone.

"Just like me, you say, just like me. I dare say, my dear Stink, there is no one just like me in the whole British Army. I have an unbroken record for successfully getting my battalion strategically lost so that we can successfully complete our missions. Missions that General Higginbottom has always felt were doomed to failure, but with my incredible military acumen, I've always succeeded. No, Stink, no one is just like me, and please do remember that. Can you remember that, Stink?" said Didlittle strictly, as he committed to memory this strange outburst from Stinkworthy, who up until now had been a useful and dutiful soldier foreman for him.

Commander Didlittle led Hawk and Doggie into the Flanagan home.

"Oh, Doggie, you're all right. Oh, thank goodness," cried Monica in delight as she rushed over to give him a big hug.

"Hello, Doggie, it's good to see you," added Matt Flanagan. "Now please do come into the drawing room and meet the rest of the family."

He introduced Didlittle and his cohorts to Mrs. Maria Flanagan, Monica, their daughter, and their two sons, nineteen-year-old Jason and his much younger brother, Bradley, who had just had his ninth birthday and who found the whole hostage-taking drama to be quite exciting, if not fun.

"Have you come to arrest the McGuintys, and are you going to put them in jail, and do you have jails small enough to hold them? Do you know they are only six inches tall?" blurted Bradley, who was keen to get his questions out before his parents told him that he was too young for grown-up conversation and not to disturb the guests.

"Bradley, you shouldn't disturb our guests with…" said Mrs. Flanagan.

But before she could finish, Didlittle interrupted her, "No, no, that's quite all right. Bradley, you are asking very intelligent questions. My answer is yes, we will arrest them, and yes, we will put them in jail, and no, we don't have any jails small enough for them. Do you have any ideas?"

Bradley pondered a moment and said, "Yes. I have a Lincoln Log cabin western frontier set that has a jailhouse that would be just the right size for them."

"Excellent!" exclaimed Didlittle. "Young man, you're going to be a big help to me. I wonder if your parents would mind if I were to recruit you into my battalion temporarily to help us get this Mc-Guinty issue settled?" he added as he turned to face the Flanagans for their approval.

The Flanagan parents turned and looked at each other and then Matt Flanagan said, "Are you sure, Commander? I mean what can a nine-year-old boy possibly do to help you with this critical mission?"

"He's already done a great deal. He's provided the jailhouse for the McGuintys, and I know he'll have a lot more good ideas before we're through. You see, Flanagan, young Bradley is still small, and he has the advantage of being able to visualize what the realities are in the small world," replied Didlittle.

"Now, as is my usual custom, I like to hear the background story to my mission in detail with a start at the beginning and preferably without interruption."

"Absolutely, Commander, excuse me," said Matt Flanagan as he turned to address his wife. "Dear, would you mind having Monica assist you in preparing some sandwiches and tea for our guests?"

"Good idea, Matt. Come along, Monica. Let's see what we can muster up for our esteemed visitors and saviours from captivity," said Maria Flanagan as she left the room with Monica.

"Come, gentlemen, sit down here by the fireplace and I'll tell you how this whole drama started." Matt ensured that his guests were comfortably settled in the large easy chairs surrounding the fireplace and then sat down himself.

"Well, let me start at the beginning."

CHAPTER 12
The McGuinty/Flanagan Relationship

"If you want to hear the whole story, at least as much as I know of it, we have to go back to the late '30s on the Isle of Dogs in the east-end of London. It was there, where two young orphan lads struck up a friendship that would last a lifetime. The two young lads were Freddy Flanagan, my father, and Mickey McGuinty, Squinty's father."

"Now, I could bore you with the details of how these very enterprising boys went on to establish a very successful grocery business by selling day-old bread and over-ripe vegetables for cut-rate prices to the poor who resided on the Isle of Dogs, but I won't."

"I could also bore you about how these boys signed up on the day World War II started and went on to be two of the most decorated soldiers in the British 8th Army fighting in North Africa and then in Europe, but I won't."

"I could bore you further by telling you that when they were discharged from the army in 1945, they decided to find a part of what remained of the British Empire that was warm and sunny all the time. I could tell you about how they went to the Royal London library and searched the British Imperial Colonial records and found that Kumquat Island was uninhabited but well-located in the warm Caribbean, but I won't."

"I could tell you of how these two brave and adventurous ex-soldiers, who saw that there was no passenger service available, managed to build and sail their own boat from London to Kumquat Island through a hurricane and arrive on its shore unharmed, but I won't."

"All I need to tell you for now is that my father, Freddie Flanagan, and Mickey McGuinty landed on Kumquat Island in 1946 and established the Kumquat Island Coffee Company, which went on to become one of the largest and finest sources of Caribbean coffee in the world."

"But, with respect, sir, it sounds like the Flanagans and the McGuintys are two very close families with that kind of history. How did your two families come to such an adversarial situation? That's a reasonable question, wouldn't you say, Commander?" asked Hawksbury as he turned to face in Didlittle's direction.

Didlittle was not in his chair but over in the corner of the room playing with Bradley and his Lincoln Log cabin set. "Sorry about that, but I wasn't paying attention. Bradley and I are building a jailhouse for the McGuintys. But do carry on," he replied.

Matt Flanagan, somewhat flummoxed by Didlittle's most unusual behaviour, continued. "That, Hawksbury, is the perplexing question that none of us have an answer for. Just a couple months ago, the two families were happily preparing for the first marriage between our two families, which we all knew would have made the two famous comrade-in-arms, Freddie and Mickey, so happy if they could have seen it. But it was not to be, as you know by now. The McGuintys were struck by this terrible curse that shrunk them, and we had to call the marriage off."

As Matt finished speaking, Mrs. Flanagan and Monica entered with an appetizing tray of tea, sandwiches, and fruit.

As Monica passed around the sandwiches, she quietly said to Doggie, "I have some dog biscuits on a side tray for you, my dear friend, Doggie."

"Oh, ruff ruff. Oh, I mean, bow wow. I mean, wow, thank you, Monica," replied Doggie.

After their tea break, the group settled in to hear Matt Flanagan continue with his story.

"Most folk believe the hostility broke out because I wouldn't let the wedding take place between our Monica and the now six-inch-tall Tobius, but that isn't quite true. Sure, the McGuintys were upset when I called off the wedding but they were upset with us before that. You see, the McGuintys have it in their mind that I placed the curse on them," Matt said as he took a sip of tea.

"With the utmost of respect, sir, did you have anything to do with the curse?" asked Hawksbury.

"Absolutely not!" answered Matt emphatically.

"Have you and Squinty tried to get to the bottom of this most unusual and, may I say, mystical event that has so dramatically changed all your lives?" asked Hawksbury.

"That's a good question and therein lies what I believe is the barrier to solving this problem," replied Matt.

"What do you think it is that prevents them from speaking to you?" asked Hawksbury.

"The McGuintys have refused to speak to us since they were shrunk by the curse. They say it is too demeaning for them to have a conversation with us now, given the huge differences in our stature. If only there was a way that I could have an eyeball-to-eyeball conversation with Squinty."

"The only way that can happen is if you were to suffer the same curse and get shrunk down to the same size as he is," replied Hawksbury.

The whole room went quiet as they contemplated the huge hazards of pursuing such a perilous course.

"Maybe not so much," said Didlittle from across the room.

"What was that?" asked Matt nervously as he was shaken out of the thought of the trauma of being shrunken down to six inches tall.

"Maybe not so much," continued Didlittle. "Bradley and I have been looking at this latest version of the Lincoln Log set that he just got for his birthday, and it includes a magical mirror that enables kids to virtually shrink down to the size of the log set, which is just about six inches."

"Really? Well tell us more about how we could use this magic mirror," said Matt.

"It's not really a magic mirror; it's just a reducing mirror that takes advantage of basic geometry. By standing at the geometric centre of the big mirror, you can be projected onto the small mirror at a height of six inches," responded Didlittle.

"That's terrific. That means we could use the mirror as a stature mediator for a meeting between Squinty and me!" exclaimed Matt.

"Correct, and we have young Bradley to thank for it, who took the trouble to read the instructions. That's remarkable for a grown man, but even more so for a nine-year-old."

"Well done, Bradley," responded all in the room. And Bradley shyly smiled but truly felt proud that he may have contributed to a way to free his family from their captivity.

CHAPTER 13
Setting a Course for a Meeting

"Well, I must admit that Bradley's magic mirror is a step towards a level-headed discussion with Squinty, but we still have to get him to agree to meet with me," said Matt.

"So the McGuintys placed your home under siege because you wouldn't let Monica marry Tobius?" asked Hawksbury.

"Yes, and Squinty also accused me of putting the spell on them that shrunk their stature," replied Matt.

"You denied it, of course?" asked Hawksbury.

"No, I considered the accusation so ludicrous I refused to respond at all."

"How long ago did he make that accusation?" asked Didlittle, now taking an interest in the conversation.

"Oh, it's been a couple of months since they put our plantation under siege," said Matt.

"And you've given him no response in all that time?" asked Didlittle.

"That's right," said Matt.

"Well, therein lies our opportunity," exclaimed Didlittle.

"I don't understand," replied Matt.

"Look here, my dear fellow. Put yourself in his shoes. Imagine you'd accused him of such a deed because you were mad at him but you weren't really sure. And imagine he doesn't respond to your accusation like you haven't. Wouldn't you be curious to hear what he had to say after all this time?"

"Yes, I suppose I would," replied Matt with a tone of growing interest in Didlittle's line of reasoning.

"Of course you would! Curiosity killed the cat and satisfaction brought him back. Now how can we get in touch with Squinty McGuinty?" asked Didlittle.

"Oh, that's easy. We've had a direct-line red phone hooked up between our two homes for over twenty years. It's only to be used in times of vital importance," replied Matt.

"Do you think he'll answer if you called him on the red phone right now?"

"Absolutely," answered Matt.

"Jolly good, then let's get you on the phone and tell Squinty that you want to speak to him immediately because you think you have an idea about what caused this trauma in the first place," suggested Didlittle.

"I do?" asked Matt.

"No, but I do," replied Didlittle. "Tell him that you'll talk about what's on your mind only if he will meet you and me in person."

"All right, where will we meet?" asked Matt.

"Good question. It should be in broad daylight in a wide open space so that neither party need fear an ambush. Let me think."

After a few minutes of quiet, Bradley spoke out. "Dad, I know a good spot to meet."

"Where?" asked Matt, who had found a new and heightened appreciation for Bradley's input.

"In the meadow by the grove of ponderosa pine trees near the front gate."

"That's perfect! Well done again, Bradley," exclaimed Matt.

"What are we waiting for? Let's call McGuinty and get the meeting set up," ordered Didlittle as he proceeded to take charge of the situation.

CHAPTER 14
The Phone Call

"This is McGuinty. I presume it's you, Flanagan, since you've called on the red phone," said Squinty gruffly.

"Given that we've known each other all our lives, could we not retain a first name basis for this conversation?" asked Matt.

"I think not. Don't forget that we're holding this plantation in a state of siege, and you are likely to remain my prisoners for the rest of your lives," responded Squinty.

"For how long?" asked Matt.

"Forever, that is unless…" Squinty hesitated and then continued. "Unless you fess up and tell me what you are up to and get this spell removed from my family," he said.

"All right, your desire to find out what's going on and to get the spell removed is understandable. I think we may have at least the beginning of an answer, if you're willing to meet with me and Commander Didlittle for a little talk."

"Didlittle! Why would I meet with Didlittle? I have no interest in meeting him and, besides, he's imprisoned in the stockade down at Refuge Beach."

"Oh, no he isn't. He's sitting right here beside me listening to this conversation," replied Matt.

"I don't believe it. Put Didlittle on the phone."

"Hello, Squinty. It's nice to hear your voice. I must say the facilities here in the Flanagan home are considerably better than what you provide down in the stockade on Refuge Beach," said Didlittle with an air of gusto.

"I don't believe it! How did you get out of the stockade? How did you get past the Beasties? How did you get into the Flanagan home?" exclaimed Squinty incredulously and with a degree of awe.

"Oh, it's all in the line of duty, my good man. I didn't get to where I am today by merely doing the expected. No, no, I got to where I am today by doing the unexpected. Isn't that right, Hawk?" asked Didlittle in a prideful and pompous tone.

"Quite right, sir," answered Hawksbury.

"Okay, okay, so why do you need to be involved in a meeting between me and Flanagan?" asked Squinty testily.

"Because my brilliant military mind is working full time on this mystery and it's soon likely to bear some results, but first we have to talk to you," answered Didlittle.

"Put Matt back on the line," barked Squinty.

"Well, Squinty, what do you say we meet for a little chat?"

"Sorry, Flanagan, but I don't hear a good enough reason to meet, and besides, why should I trust you?" answered Squinty warily.

Didlittle took the phone from Matt and said, "Squinty, you have, I think, good reason to be leery about meeting with us. How about, as a good will gesture, I agree to your men returning my troop along with Stinkworthy to the stockade?"

"Why would you want to do that?" asked Squinty cautiously.

"To show you that we believe you're a man of honour and that maybe you'll see this as a sign of good faith for a meeting."

"Put Matt back on the line," said Squinty gruffly.

"I'm back on the line, Squinty. What do you say to a meeting?" asked Matt.

"Okay, but do we have to have Didlittle involved? He gives me a headache!"

"I'm afraid so. He's the one that's driving this ship at the moment," replied Matt.

"Okay, where shall we meet?"

"How about the meadow near the ponderosas by the front gate at noon tomorrow?" asked Matt.

"Fine, see you there," responded Squinty.

CHAPTER 15
Getting Acquainted

The next day, just as Commander Didlittle's bionic watch was striking 5 pm Greenwich time, he and Matt walked into the meadow for their meeting with Squinty, but he was nowhere to be seen.

"Where could Squinty be? It's so unlike him to be late for anything," said Matt with a worried look on his face.

"Maybe he didn't understand the exact location of the meeting place," replied Didlittle.

"Are you kidding? Squinty and I played in this meadow as kids. His favourite location was under those ponderosa pine trees over there," stated Matt with certainty.

Just then a voice called out. "Hey, Flanagan, over here."

"What? That's Squinty's voice, but…"

"Hey, Flanagan, over here," and as Matt raised his line of sight, he saw Squinty McGuinty sitting up on a high bough of the tallest ponderosa.

Matt and Didlittle walked over to the foot of the tree. "Hello, Squinty. I might have known. You always loved this tree grove. You must feel comfortable in this location."

"I do, especially with me being up here and you down there."

"I don't know why you've developed this distrust in me. We've been best friends all our lives. Your attitude is a real mystery to me."

"You want a mystery, I'll give you a mystery. Why has my family been shrunk to the size of chipmunks? And just before the wedding. Now that is a mystery. You obviously don't know anything about mysteries."

"Now, now, gentlemen. Let's not get into an argument before we get started," said Didlittle. "It's very interesting that you've both zeroed in on the key element of this whole trauma and what intrigued me right from the start."

"And what might that be, Didlittle?" said Squinty testily.

"Mystery! This whole drama is a mystery. You two are partners and life-long friends, right? Yet out of nowhere, Squinty and his family are shrunk and you both have had seeds of suspicion planted in your heads. Don't you think these occurrences might be more than just coincidental? Have either of you thought that there might be some plot behind these events?"

"What are you getting at, Didlittle?" asked Squinty.

"My guardian ghost, Canterbury, says that most coincidences are usually the result of some hidden strategy of an unknown force."

"Who the dickens is Canterbury?" asked Squinty in an aggressive tone.

"Oh, never mind Canterbury for now. I think we'll need to talk about him soon enough. My point is that there is a huge chance that the developments on this island and your respective responses of animosity towards each other are part of a bigger conspiracy."

"What kind of conspiracy?" asked Matt.

"Well, I don't know, but let's ask the question: would anyone benefit from your partnership breaking up?"

"That's an interesting question. You know, Squinty, there's been considerable interest by the big coffee people since we started winning all the awards for best coffee in most classes," said Matt.

"Yes, that's true. Interesting, interesting. So you think this predicament may have been created by a big coffee merchant who wants to take over the Kumquat Coffee plantation? Is that what you're saying, Didlittle?" asked Squinty.

"I'm not saying anything. I'm merely applying my superior military intelligence questioning strategy. You two are the ones who are coming up with the answers," replied Didlittle.

"You know, Didlittle, I haven't had much use for you since your arrival on the island. But I must admit you may well be on to something," said Squinty.

"The pieces seem to fit, all right. What do you say, Squinty? How about if we put our heads together with Didlittle and see if we can get to the bottom of this conspiracy?"

"All right, but on one condition."

"What's that?"

"That we only meet at this tree. I don't want to be beside you guys physically with my shrunken stature."

Didlittle was about to mention Bradley's magic mirror but decided to hold back that information with the thought that it still may come in handy sometime later on. "That sounds all right to me. How about you, Matt?"

"That sounds okay to me. Now where do we start, Didlittle?"

CHAPTER 16
The Hypothesis

"**W**ell, let's continue the line of thinking that we started," said Didlittle.

"You mean about how a big coffee company might want to push us off the island?" asked Squinty.

"Well, sure. What do you think about that possibility, Matt?" asked Didlittle.

"I've never given it a thought until now, but there may be something to it. I don't know where that takes us."

"Don't worry about the strategic direction of this discussion. That's my responsibility. You know I didn't get to where I am today without having a superb military strategic mind."

"Okay, okay, okay. We hear you, Didlittle," replied Squinty painfully.

"Good, then let me continue my strategic questioning to see how much vital information you two already know but don't know that you know, if you know what I mean?"

"Oh, brother, this is painful," responded Squinty.

"Squinty, we seem to be making some progress. Why don't we let Didlittle carry on?" asked Matt.

"Okay, okay," replied Squinty.

"Carrying on then, over the past year has either of you seen any unusual events or, say, received any usual visitors to the island?"

Matt and Squinty remained quiet for a few moments thinking back over the year. Then Squinty said, "Hey, Matt, remember those two fellows who came ashore from their big yacht last fall when they lost their bearings and ended up staying with us for nearly a week?"

"Yes, I remember them, but what about them?"

"Don't you remember they asked a lot of questions for a couple of lost tourists? And most of all, remember how they always asked each of us the same questions, as if they were verifying everything we said? Remember how odd we thought they were with their intense interest in how we planted and harvested our beans?"

"Yes, I do remember. They were so interested in every detail of our operation, even in how we roasted the beans. That was unusual, I'd agree. But where does that take us?"

"Tuh, tuh, tuh, you leave the questions to me, Matt," responded Didlittle, who continued his questioning. "In the following months, did you receive any unexpected phone calls, faxes, or letters?"

"We received the occasional question of our interest to sell because of the outstanding reputation of the Kumquat Island coffee, but we never treated the inquiries seriously. But, wait a minute, that letter we received last year form Daddybeans Coffee was pretty aggressive. It offered a very attractive price for the company. Remember that one, Squinty? We had fun talking about how, if we sold, we'd each be able to afford to buy a comfortable condo in Manhattan and send the kids to Ivy League schools but that the kids would run away and return to the island."

"Yes, I remember, and quite frankly, the offer was way beyond anything I'd ever expected we'd get for this plantation. But you know, the most interesting part about that offer was that they sent that follow-up letter and said if the offer wasn't enough, we could name our price and they would pay it. It sounded as if Daddybeans Coffee was desperate to get their hands on our company," said Squinty.

"You're right, Squinty. Looking back, they did sound desperate, but we just had fun with it. Remember, we suggested that we'd let them have the island if their offer included the island of Manhattan."

"How did Daddybeans Coffee react to your lack of interest in their incredible offer?" asked Didlittle.

"They gave us a very unusual response, which we didn't quite understand at the time," said Matt.

"And what was that?"

"They said they were very sorry that we wouldn't sell but not as sorry as we would be," replied Matt.

"Did you take that as a threat at the time?" inquired Didlittle.

"Not really, we took it as sour grapes. You see, Didlittle, in business, big companies are trying to buy smaller companies all the time. And when they can't, they get frustrated and even angry. But they get over it in a couple days and move on to other smaller fish that may not be quite so resistant to the temptation of the rewards of a buy-out," explained Squinty.

"Sounds like the life of survival of the sea," said Didlittle.

"Precisely, and our fathers were fending off these big coffee companies for many years before they handed control over to us. So the sour grapes letter just sounded like another sour grapes letter," replied Squinty.

"But in light of the unusual events on this island recently, maybe it was more than just sour grapes. Maybe it was an ominous warning that went unheeded," said Didlittle solemnly.

Matt and Squinty remained silent, contemplating what Didlittle had just said.

Finally, Squinty said, "So what? So what if it was more than sour grapes? So what if it was a letter of warning? So what were we supposed to do? What are we supposed to do now?"

"Tuh, tuh, tuh, Squinty. Remember, I'm the one who is asking the questions. Let's not get ahead of ourselves, shall we. Always remember that I didn't get to where I am today by not being able to ask the key strategic questions," stated Didlittle sternly.

"Okay, okay. Carry on, Didlittle," responded Squinty in exasperation.

"Well, following the strict military intelligence practice, I'd say we now have enough information input to put forward a hypothesis," said Didlittle.

"I'm not sure where you're going, Didlittle, but continue," responded Squinty.

"Well, a hypothesis is an assumption made for the sake of argument. So continuing on this track, let's assume that the letter, the signals you each received to not trust the other, and the curse on the McGuintys are all related," said Didlittle.

"Okay, so suppose they are. It's not impossible," responded Matt.

"Right, so if they are related, right off the bat that can spell out the potential for good news for the McGuintys," suggested Didlittle.

"How so?" asked Squinty with a sudden burst of interest.

"Well, in the Royal Imperial book of curseology, with which I am very familiar, there are only two kinds of curses," continued Didlittle.

"Wait a minute. Why would a military man be well-versed on curseology?" asked Squinty.

"There's a good reason for that, but that can wait. Now as I was saying, there are two kinds of curses. One is the random curse that can afflict anyone at anytime. This one is very hard to deal with as its source is almost never known. Usually, the only treatment is prayer and good behaviour, which, when put together, is referred to as grace. It basically comes about when the afflicted person chooses to live their life as best they can without looking for sympathy or special favours. These people usually seem to glow in the eyes of those who are close. This kind of person survives with style and dignity and they are said to have grace," said Didlittle.

"That sounds reasonable. What about the other kind of curse?" inquired Squinty with heightening curiosity.

"The other kind of curse is the ghostly curse."

"What's the difference?" asked Matt.

"The difference is that it is a curse that is placed by a specific ghost, which means that if one can get to that ghost, there's a possibility to have it removed."

"Now you're talking, Didlittle. Let's get a hold of this ghost and have this curse lifted!" responded Squinty vigorously.

"I'm afraid it's not quite that easy, Squinty," said Didlittle.

"It's not? Why not?"

"Because to get the curse removed, you have to track down the ghost who placed it and that can take a long time. In fact, without the proper strategic approach and some luck, it can take forever and still the ghost can't be found," responded Didlittle.

"So there's some hope, but not much, of my family getting rid of this curse. Is that what you're saying, Didlittle?"

"Oh, Squinty, you always read a little too much or a little too little into what I say. Listen carefully to what I'm going to say. I said without a proper strategic approach, finding the ghost would be difficult. But you're lucky enough to have Commander Didlittle, famous leader of the Lost Battalion, well-known for a keen eye for strategy, at your service."

"Okay, Didlittle. Keep talking," said Squinty with the air of resignation of one who knows he's going to hear it all anyway.

"Right, now thinking strategically, what do we have from our hypothesis? We have the basic assumption that these events are all related to your negative reply to the Daddybeans Coffee Company. If so, then someone with them or someone contracted by them would have arranged the spell. Does this make sense so far?" asked Didlittle.

"Yes, yes," replied both Squinty and Matt in unison.

"Good, then let's take it a step farther. The spell has been in place for about two months now and neither of you have indicated to the Daddybeans Coffee Company that you want to sell. Is that so?" asked Didlittle.

"Absolutely not. We'd never sell to them, would we, Matt?"

"No, never," replied Matt.

"Right, so now put yourself in their shoes. Wouldn't you be curious to find out what's going on at the Kumquat Island Coffee Company after the spell's been in place for two months?" asked Didlittle.

"Well, sure, we probably would, but how could we do that?" asked Matt.

"By employing an elementary procedure that's called covert agent placement. It's a standard military tactic."

"I think what you're saying is that they would send an under-cover agent onto the island. Is that right?" asked Squinty.

"Bingo! That's precisely what I'm saying," replied Didlittle.

"But who can it be?" asked Matt.

"I've already got a good idea," said Didlittle with a measure of satisfaction.

"Who?" exclaimed Matt and Squinty in unison.

"Well, it's only a hypothesis at the moment, so we must be care-ful not to over-react to what I'm going to say. I believe that if our hypothesis is true, then a good candidate for the undercover agent is none other than Sergeant-Major Stinkworthy."

"But if that's true, why did you send him back to Refuge Beach? He might get away!" exclaimed Squinty.

"Oh, don't worry about that. He's not going anywhere. You see, I've been suspicious of Stink since our first meeting. He's committed a couple of small and barely noticeable errors regarding military protocol, errors so small that most other British officers might not have noticed. But I noticed because I know precisely how a Sergeant-Major must act and speak. You see, I was once a Sergeant-Major myself."

"So why did you send him back to Refuge Beach?"

"Because I set a trap for him that will achieve two things. First, it will confirm beyond any shadow of a doubt that he is an undercover agent, as you call him. Second, it will provide us with a vehicle to manipulate him and the Daddybeans Coffee Company."

"Splendid! You know, Didlittle, I may have underestimated your talents as a British Officer."

"Don't feel bad, Squinty. Most people do until they see what a brilliant Commander I really am."

"Okay, okay, Didlittle, enough already. I knew I shouldn't have paid you that complement," responded Squinty.

"All right, that's enough for today. We'll re-group here again tomorrow at the same time. Hopefully, by then, Stink will have taken the bait and I'll have some very interesting news for you."

CHAPTER 17
Hypothesis Confirmed

Meanwhile, several miles down the plantation road leading back to Refuge Beach, Stinkworthy marched in front of the troop. But his heart wasn't in it. He was brooding over why Commander Didlittle suddenly cut him loose just when he thought he'd done a good job of working into his good graces.

As he walked along, he saw a curious-looking piece of paper attached to a tree at eye-level, simply imprinted "STINKWORTHY." He marched past it and told the drummer sergeant, who held the highest rank in the troop, to keep on marching. He then doubled back, tore the note off the tree, and turned it over. On the other side, it read:

"Stinkworthy, Destroy this note after reading. There is a cell phone behind this tree. Use it to phone 1-800-465-3432 and recite all the details you have so far into the voicemail. This information will be passed on to the key person at Daddybeans Coffee Company. Also, listen carefully, as you will receive instructions for your next move. Good luck. Destroy this message after committing to memory."

Stinkworthy looked about to be sure no one was looking and quickly picked up the cell phone from behind the tree, stuffed it into his pocket, and then marched swiftly after the troop to get back to the front.

After being returned to the stockade and the marching band troop was sequestered with the rest of the Lost Battalion, Stinkworthy found a bush to stand behind and dialled the number on the cell phone.

"Hello, Stinkworthy. This is your contact person from the Daddybeans Coffee Company. Please press # and leave a message every twenty-four hours stating all that you've learned so far with your undercover work, then press * to receive further instructions," said the message on the cell phone.

Stinkworthy then pressed the # key and proceeded to give a full description of what he'd seen so far on Kumquat Island. He finished up by saying, "A new, unexpected development was the arrival of Commander Didlittle and his Lost Battalion yesterday. He's a pompous nincompoop with an over-inflated opinion of himself, and he continuously gets his battalion lost. He's a pleasant enough chap, and if he wasn't so pathetic, he'd almost be likeable. He's nothing to worry about, though. He spends so much time with self-complements, he doesn't pay attention to what's going on around him. He really thinks I'm a Sergeant-Major, and I've got him completely fooled. We'll be able to play him for a fool as we gather the intelligence we need to take over the Kumquat Island Coffee Company."

CHAPTER 18
The Icebreaker Plan

The next day at noon, Didlittle and Matt hiked up to the base of the large ponderosa tree and cordially greeted Squinty, who was perched up on a high bough.

"Good day, Squinty. We have some very interesting news to share with you," announced Didlittle cheerfully.

"But before we go into that, did you receive an unusual letter yesterday?" asked Matt.

"Yes, I did. It was a copy of the letter that was sent to you," replied Squinty.

"Then you know it said that if you and I didn't agree to sell the company to Daddybeans Coffee Company within five days, all the Flanagans would be shrunken to your size and that they'd come in and take over the company and not pay us anything!"

"Yes, I'm aware of that. This certainly confirms Didlittle's hypothesis."

"Okay, Squinty, now listen to this tape," said Didlittle.

A few minutes later, after hearing the tape of Stinkworthy's voicemail message from the planted cell phone, Squinty said, "Well, I'll be darned; this has been the work of Daddybeans Coffee right from the start. Didlittle, this is great news and means we'll soon be able to get back to living normally again."

"Not so fast, Squinty. We've still got a lot of investigative military intelligence work ahead. It's true that we've made great strides by confirming the hypothesis about Daddybeans Coffee. But we still have to find a way to remove the spell from your family and that means we have to determine the source of the spell. If and when we find that out, we'll then have to find a way to get to that source, and that won't be easy. And that letter tells us we've only got five days to do all this," replied Didlittle with a serious tone.

"So we're not out of the woods yet," replied Squinty.

"Not yet, but we've made a lot of progress in the last day, and I expect we'll make a lot more in the next twenty-four hours," said Didlittle.

"So, what's next?" asked Matt.

"Well, gentlemen, we've got Stink set up to do our dirty work for us, and now we'll put him to work without him even knowing it."

"Didlittle, could you please explain exactly what you mean?" asked Squinty.

"Of course. Here's what the next step will be," said Didlittle in a secretive tone. "You see, the key to military intelligence work is finding a way to extract all the vital information that you can from your enemy when you get the chance. Now that we've got Stink set up, we have the chance to extract all the intelligence about Daddybeans' nasty plot that we can and, hopefully, find the source of the McGuinty spell."

"That sounds pretty complicated. Where would you even start?" inquired Matt with awe.

"We simply follow strict military intelligence procedures, add a dash of Didlittle imagination, and we should do just fine. The situation we have here calls for an icebreaker. Now, I know that term refers to a polite way to start a conversation in a social setting, but in military terms, it means something else entirely. In military intelligence, an icebreaker refers to a method where the enemy agent, in our case, Stinkworthy, is fed misinformation that will stimulate him to unwittingly disclose confidential information to us. And that's what we're going to do."

"But how, where, who...?" inquired Squinty, showing a high interest in the unfolding intrigue.

"That will all be revealed in the anti-agent icebreaker plan that we'll go over now."

CHAPTER 19
The Bait is Taken

The next day, Stinkworthy slowly wandered about the stockade and checked to make sure no one was watching him. He then ducked in behind the same bush and called the cell phone voicemail to report no new developments and listened to his instructions.

"Stinkworthy, you are doing excellent undercover work. Your report right from Kumquat Island is invaluable to us. We're very interested to hear that Commander Didlittle is nothing but a nincompoop and that you have him completely fooled. Well done!"

"Now, we have had reports from other parts of the island that some of the McGuintys are starting to grow. This is disturbing, as it might mean that the spell is starting to wear off. As you can well imagine, if that were to happen before we can coerce the McGuintys and Flanagans to sell, our entire nasty plot will have failed. We thought the spell was to last for a year, but maybe we made a mistake when we requested it. Do you have any advice on how we can be sure we got a one-year spell put on the McGuintys? We look forward to hearing your reply."

Stinkworthy stared at the dark waters of Caffeine Lake, whose edge was only a few feet away. He wondered how the Daddybeans Coffee Company could hire such dimwitted criminal agents. There's no way the spell would wear off so fast. He definitely ordered a one-year spell, and he was certain that's what the McGuintys got! The more Stinkworthy thought about the voicemail, the more irritated he became.

Rather than taking the time to reflect on what would be the most secure way of replying to safeguard against possible infiltration of his communication to the agents for Daddybeans Coffee, he immediately went back behind the bush, called the given number on the cell phone, and left the following message:

"In response to your voicemail about the McGuintys starting to grow, let me assure you that there is and has been no sign of that in all the time I've been on Kumquat Island. Also, let me assure you that I definitely ordered a one-year spell from the ghost of Gaston Y Goatwich, who has always complied with my orders. I would be shocked, yes, shocked if the McGuinty spell was not precisely as I ordered. With respect, I await furthers instructions. Stinkworthy."

CHAPTER 20
Where's Canterbury?

The next day at noon, Didlittle and Matt walked out to the meadow and noticed that Squinty was sitting on a much lower bough on the tree.

"Good day, Squinty. I see that you're sitting on a lower bough. Does that mean you're starting to trust us, perhaps?" asked Didlittle.

"Perhaps, but I won't trust anybody until my family gets restored to their proper size," said Squinty sternly.

"Well, Squinty, we have some interesting information to share with you. Listen to this," said Didlittle as he turned on the tape of Stinkworthy's most recent voicemail. After a few moments of listening to the tape, Didlittle turned it off.

"The ghost of Gaston Y Goatwich?" asked Squinty.

"Bingo!" said Didlittle.

"What do you know about the ghost of Gaston Y Goatwich?" inquired Matt.

"Nothing at the moment," replied Didlittle.

"Then we're back where we started," Squinty said glumly.

"Not quite. I said I knew nothing at the moment, but that doesn't mean I can't find out a lot with the application of the resources at my disposal," replied Didlittle.

"What resources could the military have that would help us with a ghost and a spell?" asked Matt.

"I didn't say military resources. I said resources at my disposal. Now before I go any further, I'm going to have to ask you both to swear a double Dutch Eagle Scout promise that you'll not tell anyone what I'm going to tell you," said Didlittle.

"A double Dutch Eagle Scout promise! That's as high as it goes. We couldn't even share this secret with a blood brother!" exclaimed Squinty, obviously impressed with the high level of the secret that Didlittle was about to reveal.

"We promise!" exclaimed both Matt and Squinty in unison, eager to hear what Didlittle had to say.

"Good, then I will tell you about Canterbury."

"Canterbury, who's that?" inquired both Matt and Squinty in unison again.

"Well, as you know, I am world famous in my ability to travel about the world doing good work for the MOOGOO department of the British Military by stopping nasty plots wherever they may be. And while it is true my success is largely based on my incredible ability to apply strict military strategic thinking to any given situation in an instant, I also have an ace up my sleeve. And that is my ghost friend, Canterbury. He always comes to provide help or valued advice whenever I have a crisis."

"You mean to tell us that you have a ghost at your beck and call?" asked Squinty.

"Yes, you might say that," Didlittle replied rather smugly.

"Are we going to be able to see him, or is he only visible to your eyes?" asked Matt with growing wonder.

"You'll be able to see him too if you recite the ghostly code for Canterbury," said Didlittle.

"And will you share that code with us?" asked Squinty.

"Yes. In fact, I'm going to recite it now to call him."

> "Hammer and Sickle,
> I am deep in a pickle,
> But I need not worry,
> As I'll just call for Canterbury
> Hicklesicklepickleticklemetoo."

A few anxious moments went by but nothing happened.

"Maybe you should recite it again," said Matt.

"I don't ever have to repeat myself; he always comes." A few more minutes and still nothing happened.

"All right, I'll recite it again," said Didlittle, but still nothing happened.

After an hour went by, with Didlittle reciting the ghost code every few minutes, Matt said, "Maybe he's just not available today."

Obviously frustrated and embarrassed, Didlittle could only continue to repeat, "I don't understand it, I don't understand it," over and over.

Finally, Squinty said, "Well, at least your cell phone idea is working. Let's meet again tomorrow at noon and see if we've made any more headway."

With the meeting over, Matt and Didlittle walked back to the Flanagan home.

CHAPTER 21
The Canterbury Advantage

Feeling dejected and humiliated, Commander Didlittle excused himself and went up to his room. After closing the door, he hung up his hat, turned towards the bed, and was shocked to see Canterbury, a wispy image of a portly, balding, rosy-cheeked monk wearing a robe with a hood and a coarse rope for a sash. He reeled back and shouted, "What are you doing here? Why didn't you come when I recited the ancient rhyme?"

"My dear Didlittle, I am not a novelty to be shown off to your friends. You must understand that I only respond when I see that you're really in a pickle with no way out. Like the time you misread your orders and parachuted into the Belgian Congo when you and your outfit were fitted out for Antarctica. Oh, you chaps were certainly overdressed for that mission, weren't you?"

"We don't need to go into that right now. If you're not going to help, then why are you here?" asked Didlittle.

"I didn't say that I wouldn't help. I said I was not going to be a novelty act for the amusement of your friends."

"Fine, what does that mean?"

"It means that I'll help you, but your friends won't be able to see me or hear me. For them, I won't exist."

"Oh, yes you will, because I'll tell them you're helping me."

"You can tell them what you want; they're not going to believe you. Did you see the looks on their faces after you called for me for

the umpteenth time and I still didn't appear? No, for them I will not exist no matter what you tell them."

"Fine, then can you, at least, help me?" asked Didlittle with an air of resignation.

"I don't know. What seems to be the problem?"

"Where should I begin?"

"Why don't you start at the beginning?"

"All right," said Didlittle and proceeded to tell Canterbury about all that had happened. He finished up with, "So the challenge is to get the spell lifted from the McGuinty family within the next five days."

"And you say the spell was cast by the ghost of Gaston Y Goatwich?"

"That's right. Does that name ring a bell?"

"No, can't say that it does. We need to know what hamlet he resides in."

"Hamlet?"

"Yes, hamlet. You see ghosts usually have a home hamlet to reside in. That is unless they're called off to some foreign land to help a lost soul, like I often do for you."

"Okay, I need to find out his home hamlet. Anything else?"

"Usually, that would be enough. But in this instance, find out if he speaks English. The name Gaston Y Goatwich sounds French."

"Okay, home hamlet and confirm he speaks English. Anything else?"

"No, that should do it."

CHAPTER 22
The Channel Islands Residence

The next day, as usual, Stinkworthy used the cell phone to report the past day's activities, which were minimal. Then he pressed * and heard his message.

"Well done, Stinkworthy. Your information is very useful to us. We need to know every detail of what is going on out there. By the way, we think we understand why the communication with your ghost wasn't so good. Isn't Gaston Y Goatwich French? That would explain why the McGuinty spell wasn't what we ordered. Please confirm if this could possibly be the reason why the orders may have been misunderstood."

On hearing this message, Stinkworthy became very angry and was tempted to toss the cell phone into Caffeine Lake.

"Why can't these guys understand my message?" Stinkworthy thought to himself.

Without hesitation, he punched a key and spoke into the cell phone. "The ghost of Gaston Y Goatwich is not French. It's true that he can speak a little patois of a French/English mixture but that's common for those who reside in the Channel Islands. His first language is English, he understands it well, and he definitely understood that the McGuinty spell order was for one year!" Stinkworthy then slammed the cell phone shut, feeling much better that he had expressed his frustration to the Daddybucks guys for not understanding him the first time.

CHAPTER 23
Channel Islands or Not

Later that evening, Didlittle played the message for Canterbury. After it was finished, Canterbury said "Ah, yes, the Channel Islands. Now there is an interesting place for a ghost hamlet."

"How so?" asked Didlittle.

"Well, the Channel Islands are a part of the UK, even though they are just off the coast of France. Because of their location, they have a lot of independence from the UK and that has attracted the, shall we say, more adventurous type of folk who don't like to be restricted by a lot of laws. Free spirits, if you will."

"Oh, Canterbury, I know all that. What's your point?"

"My point is that ghosts resemble the people who reside in their hamlets. Therefore, the ghost of Gaston Y Goatwich will very likely be what I would call a free spirit."

"Is that good or bad?"

"That depends. Most of the people there are law-abiding and just like the freedom of the island way of life. But there are some people who are there because they can avoid the law. Some of those people are involved in nasty business. And, of course, the same would hold true for the ghosts there."

"This is getting too complicated. All we're trying to do is get the spell on the McGuintys lifted. Why is all this stuff about the Channel Islands important to us?" asked Didlittle.

"Because you are going to have to go there."

"What! I can't leave Kumquat Island. I have my mission to complete, and I have my battalion down at Refuge Beach to look after," said Didlittle with concern.

"Didlittle, you know that ghost transport gets you anywhere in a matter of seconds. You won't be off the island for long. And besides, you can leave Hawksbury in charge."

"Canterbury, you obviously do not understand the high level of responsibility I have as the Commanding Officer of the Lost Battalion. I cannot leave my men. And that's final!" exclaimed Didlittle.

"Fine, then I'll get back to my hamlet and continue my gardening, which I was enjoying immensely before you interrupted me."

"What, you're just going to leave me. You're not going to help me lift the spell. What kind of a guardian ghost are you?"

"I'm the best you'll ever see. I've offered to help, but your refusal to go to the Channel Islands prevents me from doing that, so I'll just say adieu."

"No, wait, I'll go with you to the Channel Islands, but first I've got to tell Matt and Squinty what we're up to. All right?" asked Didlittle pleadingly.

"Okay, you leave tomorrow right after you meet with them," replied Canterbury with an air of impatience.

CHAPTER 24
The Channel Islands

The next morning, when the Flanagan residence awoke, there was a fierce tropical storm raging across the island.

"We won't be able to meet Squinty out at the ponderosa tree today, Commander Didlittle. Should I call him on the red phone and cancel the meeting?" asked Matt.

"Definitely not. I have to leave for the Channel Islands as soon as possible, and it's important that Squinty knows our next move so we don't lose his trust."

"But we can't meet out at the ponderosa tree in this foul weather," exclaimed Matt.

"Right, and your son Bradley and I have devised a way for Squinty to meet with us in the back room and out of the weather using Bradley's magic mirror. Bradley, why don't you lead us out to the back room and show us how the mirror will work," said Didlittle.

"Okay! Everybody follow me," said Bradley, obviously very excited to show off his expertise with the magic mirror.

After the scientific principle of the magic mirror was explained for the adults, Bradley was invited to stay for the meeting with Squinty. Matt then called Squinty and explained the mirror and suggested that Squinty come to the house and use it to appear full-sized for the meeting. Squinty was initially sceptical but agreed to come when told that Didlittle had some exciting news to report.

Once Bradley had explained the principle of the mirror and showed Squinty how to use it to appear full-sized to everyone present, the meeting got underway.

Again, Didlittle began the meeting by playing the tape of Stinkworthy's most recent voicemail message.

"So, we now know that the ghost resides in the Channel Islands. That's where I'll have to go to see this ghost and get the spell lifted," said Didlittle.

"The Channel Islands! It will take weeks, if not months to get there and back," exclaimed Squinty.

"When you travel by way of ghost transport, it only takes a few seconds," responded Didlittle.

"Oh, brother. We're not going to go through that ghost thing again, are we?" Squinty asked.

"Do you believe your shrinkage was a spell?" asked Didlittle.

"Yes."

"Do you believe that a spell comes from the extrasensory world?"

"Yes."

"Then you shouldn't have much difficulty believing in the existence of ghosts," said Didlittle.

"I'm not having that much difficulty with the possibility of ghosts, but I have just one question."

"What's that?"

"How come you can't produce Canterbury for us all to see?"

"That's a long story, but never mind. Here's the plan I've worked out for our next steps."

CHAPTER 25
The Channel Island Visit

Bradley couldn't believe his good fortune. Here he was on a major mission with Commander Didlittle. Even though his mom and dad had agreed to let Didlittle recruit him temporarily into his charge back on Kumquat Island, he only thought Didlittle wanted his advice about small things and people, like the McGuintys. Now he was walking down the main street of a town somewhere in the Channel Islands, moving as fast as he could to keep up with Didlittle, who was walking brusquely like a man with a purpose.

"How did you like your first try at ghost transport, Bradley?"

"It was cool, Commander Didlittle, but it only seemed to take a brief moment to get all the way from Kumquat Island to here."

"Yes, that's the advantage of ghost transport; it saves a lot of time."

"Commander Didlittle, can I ask you a question?"

"Of course, Bradley. What is it?"

"Why didn't you bring one of the others? Why did you bring me?"

"Because I could only bring someone who believed in me and who I could trust. Squinty wouldn't qualify on either count. Your Dad is someone that I could trust, but I don't think he believed me when I spoke about Canterbury."

"What about Hawksbury? You can trust him, and he believes in you."

"Quite right, Bradley, quite right. I could have brought Hawk, that's true, but I needed him to stay on Kumquat Island to take charge of the battalion while I was away."

Bradley walked along silently, letting Didlittle's remarks sink in.

"You see, Bradley, we're now on an active assignment that could get pretty dicey before we're done, so I need someone with me whom I can trust. But in order to be able to travel on ghost transport, one has to believe not only in me, but also, and more importantly, in Canterbury. As Canterbury always says, 'If you don't believe in the ghost, then don't expect him to be your host!' So, Bradley, aside from Hawk, you were the only one I could bring. Now do you understand why you're here?"

"Yes, I do, and may I say thank you for the privilege to be here."

"Enough of that; we've got some serious investigative work ahead of us. Our first stop is the land registry office for the Channel Islands. That's why we're here on the Island of Jersey. Ah, here we are: 23435 High Street. This is the place. Let's go in, shall we?"

After opening a heavy, old, dark brown swinging door, the two walked up a short flight of stairs. The office walls were all dark brown wood with green blinds on the windows. The place felt and smelled like an old library or museum. Didlittle approached the lady behind the counter and said, "Good morning, madam. I wonder if you could tell me where we might find the hamlet of Gaston Y Goatwich?"

"Yes, it's located on Guernsey Island, but it gets very few visitors these days."

"And why is that?"

"Oh, it sounds silly, but they say it has a ghost."

"Perfect!"

"Excuse me, what was that?"

"Oh, never mind. Can you please tell us how to get there?"

"Why yes, there's a daily ferry to Guernsey that sails in about twenty minutes, and if you hurry, you should still make it."

"Excellent! Which way to the ferry?"

"Turn left out the door and go down to the end of this block, turn left and the ferry slip is right there. Now get along if you wish to catch that ferry!"

"Thank you very much, madam. Come along, Bradley. We haven't a moment to spare," yelled Didlittle as he rushed out the door.

As they ran onto the ferry landing, there were two ferries preparing to sail.

"I don't see any signs. Oh, never mind, we'll board the big one. That should be the one going to Guernsey, since it's the bigger island."

"Oh, Commander Didlittle, that's so clever. I would have wasted time and gone back to ask the lady which ferry to catch."

"It's what you call instinct, Bradley. It's like another sense, and it saves a lot of time. But you only get it with extensive experience in military intelligence."

As they settled onto a seat on the top deck to enjoy the warm, sunny day, they heard "Now hear this, now hear this. Welcome aboard everybody. Our sailing time to the island of St. Anne will be six hours. We expect some choppy weather, so please come inside once we've cleared the harbour."

Didlittle was startled to hear the ferry was sailing to St. Anne and not Guernsey Island. He rushed up to a ferry officer and said, "Where's the ferry to Guernsey?" The officer pointed to the smaller ferry that was also just pulling out of its slip.

"How can that ferry be going to Guernsey? It's smaller and Guernsey is a much bigger island than St. Anne."

"Because our trip to St. Anne is much longer and it takes us out into the English Channel, where we get more of a sea. That's why we have a bigger ferry."

Didlittle turned to Bradley and said, "Come with me on the double."

As the two run back up to the top deck, Didlittle said, "It's a good thing I noticed where the lifeboat station was," as he removed a fire axe, broke open the rescue locker, and removed a long rope with a grappling hook on the end.

"Stand back," yelled Didlittle as he threw the grappling hook across the water to hook onto the railing of the smaller ferry.

"Okay, Bradley, we have no time to waste. We must make contact with Gaston Y Goatwich as soon as possible. It's too late for both of us to disembark and catch the Guernsey ferry, as they are lifting their ramp as we speak. There won't be another one until tomorrow, and we can't wait that long to make contact with Gaston. I have secured this lifeline to the Guernsey ferry with the grappling hook so that you can slide right down onto its deck. Go over the side of this ferry, slide down the rope, and pull yourself onto that ferry," Didlittle said as he pointed to the smaller ferry, which was just about to pull away from its slip.

"Here's twenty-five pounds for sustenance. You'll need it. When you get off the ferry, look for the Watering Hole Pub. The owner's name is Paddy, and he's an old friend of mine. Ask him to put you up for the night."

"First thing tomorrow, walk around the hamlet and ask about the ghost. Let it be known that you're looking for Gaston Y Goatwich. If he's there, he'll find you. Tell him his old friend Canterbury sent you and me, but I was unavoidably delayed. Ask him if he'd mind lifting the spell as a favour to Canterbury."

"When you're finished, return to the Watering Hole Pub, and I will meet you there. You are the only chance we have of getting to Gaston Y Goatwich in time to get the McGuintys freed from the spell. Now go, as the ferries are going to start moving apart in a few more seconds!"

Bradley nervously started to shinny along the rope. After a few feet, he looked down and realized that he was suspended between two ferries about to depart, he was a good fifty feet above the water, and he couldn't swim. He froze, unable to move any muscles at all.

CHAPTER 26
Keep Moving

"Don't stop, Bradley. Keep moving," cried Didlittle.

"I can't move; I think I'm frozen with fear."

"What are you afraid of?"

"If I fall into the ocean, I'll probably drown because I can't swim."

"Bradley, if you fall into the ocean, the ferries will run over you, so swimming wouldn't help, anyway. Now get going, and that's an order!"

The clarity and sternness of Didlittle's voice shook Bradley out of his fear freeze, and he quickly shinned his way to the other ferry. Just as he climbed over the railing, both ferries pulled away from their slips and the rope snapped like a string.

As the ferries headed away in different directions, Bradley had a thought and yelled to Didlittle, "What if Gaston Y Goatwich doesn't want to lift the spell?" But by this time the ferries were so far apart that Didlittle couldn't hear him.

CHAPTER 27
A Friend in Need

By the time the ferry pulled into Guernsey, the weather had changed drastically. A storm had blown in from Iceland and the rain was driven into Bradley's face as he disembarked from the ferry. The heavy, dark clouds overhead reminded Bradley that evening was fast approaching, and he realized that he was very hungry. Noticing that the stores were all closed, Bradley concluded that the business hours were over for the day, so any office inquiries about Gaston Y Goatwich would have to wait until tomorrow.

With Commander Didlittle's instructions in mind, Bradley had asked people on the ferry about the location of the Watering Hole Pub. He was happy to hear that it was only two doors down the street from the ferry dock.

He remembered his parents saying that a UK pub was a good place for getting a decent, inexpensive meal and to find out what was going on in the community. Although Bradley understood that there is no age restriction for guests going into a pub, he still felt pretty nervous when he walked into The Watering Hole Pub.

A lad his age walking into a pub unattended would catch one's eye anywhere. On a remote island like Guernsey, where the patrons all knew each other and where strangers are rare, a young chap like Bradley caught everyone's eye.

By now, Bradley was more than nervous, he was scared, but he remembered Didlittle saying before they departed that he was the only chance of getting the curse lifted before the Flanagans got afflicted by the same curse.

Not being sure what to do now that he was inside the pub, he remembered his mom saying to him that whenever one is in a tight spot, just telling the plain truth would never hurt.

"Can I help you, laddie?" asked the bartender in a deep but not unfriendly voice.

"Yes, please. I'm looking for Paddy," replied Bradley.

At the mention of Paddy's name, a hush fell over the entire pub.

"Well, I am so sorry, son, but Paddy was in a motorcycle accident last month and had to be flown to London for special care. Is there anything I can do for you?"

Bradley lingered a moment longer, thinking about his mom's advice and decided to go with it.

"Yes, sir, that is, I hope so, sir. My name is Bradley Flanagan. I came from Kumquat Island and my family are partners with the McGuinty family in the Kumquat Island Coffee Company. I came here to seek out the ghost of Gaston Y Goatwich to see if we can arrange the removal of a curse that was placed on our partners, the McGuintys, but I don't have much time."

"So you came all this way to find a ghost, did you?" said the bartender amid howls of laughter throughout the pub.

Bradley could feel his cheeks turning red. He was so embarrassed he didn't know what to say. He wished he was back home with his friends and family at that moment.

"Kumquat Island Coffee Company, you say?" asked a motherly voice from the far side of the pub.

"Yes, ma'am," Bradley replied nervously.

"Well, lad, we've tasted your coffee in the finest coffee houses in London, and it's mighty fine. Why don't you come over here and join us, and we'll stand you a glass of lemonade. You like lemonade, don't you?"

"Yes, ma'am."

"Good, then come over and join us."

As Bradley slowly approached the table, a tall, athletic-looking man with a friendly face stood and extended his hand. "My name is Andrew Steele and I'm glad to make your acquaintance. This is my wife, Kathryn Steele."

"I'm glad to meet you. My name is Bradley."

"Flanagan, we know, you just introduced yourself to the whole pub. Now do sit down."

Once Bradley was comfortably settled in his chair, Mrs. Steele said, "Are you related to the renowned and well-decorated private Flanagan who fought with the 8th Army in North Africa during World War II?"

"Yes, he was my grandfather."

"Well, then we're almost related. You see, my father also fought with the 8th Army in North Africa, and I can remember him returning home and telling us all these astounding stories about the brave exploits of his good friend Flanagan. As I recall, there was another person who shared in those exploits and was equally decorated by the King."

"You must mean Mr. McGuinty."

"Yes, that's the name. Whatever became of those two?"

By now the novelty of Bradley's appearance had worn off, and the patrons went back to their own conversations about the soccer finals and the need for higher taxes on the rich, who were moving onto the islands and spoiling the way of life for the local folk.

"With your permission, ma'am, I will tell you the whole story about the McGuintys and the Flanagans. It will take some time, but it will bring you right up to the present and why I'm here seeking the ghost of Gaston Y Goatwich. That is, if you have the time?"

"Oh, yes, please, do tell," said Mr. and Mrs. Steele in unison.

After telling the whole story, starting with the formation of the grocery business by his grandfather and Mr. McGuinty all the way through to the current situation on Kumquat Island, Bradley finished up by saying, "And that's it."

"So that's why a young tyke like you is here on Guernsey Island on your own?" asked Mr. Steele.

"Yes, sir. That's about it, sir."

"Well, it doesn't sound like your Commander Didlittle is very clever to me."

"Oh, Mr. Steele, with respect, sir, Commander Didlittle is very clever. He commands an entire battalion of MOOGOO, the elite British Intelligence unit that fights crime and corruption all over the world. He just got the ferries mixed up, and that can happen to anyone."

"All right, so what's your plan of action for finding this Gaston Y Goatwich?"

"I don't have one, sir."

"You don't have a plan of action?"

"Not really."

"Well then, we'd better develop one."

"Yes, sir, but may I ask you a question?"

"Of course, laddie. What is it?"

"Why would you two want to get involved in this?"

"Two reasons: We are fascinated by the subject of ghost haunting, and we have two sons who are not much older than you. We'd like to think that they'd get assistance if they were in a jam in a far away land. Now let's dispense with the formalities. I'll call you Bradley and you can call us Andrew and Kathryn."

"Oh, sir, I could never call you two Andrew and Kathryn."

"Well, we don't want to be called Mr. and Mrs. Steele. It's too formal and it makes us feel old."

"I've got it. Why don't you call us Mr. and Mrs. S.?" suggested Mrs. Steele.

"Okay."

"Good, so we got that settled. Now let's see what Harry our bartender knows about Gaston Y Goatwich."

Mr. S. called Harry over to their table and said, "Tell me, Harry, what's the story out at the manor of Gaston Y Goatwich?"

"I can't tell you too much. Very few of the local folk go out there. They're spooked by the place."

"Why is that?"

"The local folk feel that it is, in fact, haunted by a ghost."

"What's the story on the ghost?"

"Don't know much. The rumour on the island is that the ghost has something to do with the fact that the Nazis were on this island during the war."

"Anything else?"

"No, not really."

"Thanks, Harry."

CHAPTER 28
Seeking Gaston Y Goatwich

The next morning, Bradley woke up and smelled the familiar and comfortable scent of brewing coffee. His trained nostrils told him the coffee was not Kumquat Island coffee, but a very good blend nevertheless.

He was very comfortable lying on the soft yet firm mattress, covered with a big fluffy eiderdown, so he just lay in the bed and reflected on last night.

Mr. and Mrs. Steele had invited him to stay with them in their condominium. It was quite large. "Large enough for me, my wife, our two sons, two dogs, and a cat," was the way Mr. S. had described it.

Mr. S. explained that he had an international contracting business, which was focused mainly on North Africa and the Middle East. The family home was in Nottingham, England, but he had to travel a lot. For some tax reason they had to reside in the Channel Islands for a fortnight every couple of months. They had this spacious condominium here in Guernsey so that the family could come on visits when school was not in session.

"Bradley, are you awake yet?" called Mrs. S.

"Yes, ma'am."

"Good, then have a shower and come down for breakfast when you've dressed."

After breakfast, Mr. S. said, "Bradley, I made a few phone calls this morning and gathered some intelligence. Apparently, the hamlet of Gaston Y Goatwich is on the far side of the island. The local folk are certain that the old seaside manor out there is haunted. So that, I suppose, is a good thing if we're looking for a ghost. However, there is a strange story tied in with this manor."

"What's that?"

"Apparently, during the war, the Nazis built a large underground network of rooms and offices that were located very deep below the surface."

"What was it used for?"

"That's where it gets mysterious. Today, it's used as a hospital, and most folk say that's what the Nazis built it for. But there are others who say the Allied forces would never have deliberately bombed a hospital and that the Nazis had other uses for an underground tunnel network."

"Like what?"

"That's the mystery."

"What has this got to do with finding the ghost of Gaston Y Goatwich?"

"I'm not sure. Maybe nothing, maybe a lot."

"Mr. S., I'm not following you."

"Well, you see, Bradley, there are some folk that say the tunnel system is connected to the manor of Gaston Y Goatwich. In fact, they claim their parents told them that the manor of Gaston Y Goatwich was known as 'Achtung, It's a Snitch' because they felt the manor was secretly used by the Nazis."

"But, for what?"

"I expect we'll need to find that out before we're through."

After breakfast, as Bradley rode along with Mr. S. at the wheel of the family car, he noticed how different the rolling countryside of Guernsey Island was from the tropical forest and mountains of Kumquat Island.

After just ten minutes, they arrived at an old manor perched on a high cliff overlooking the sea. Alighting from the car, they approached the front entrance to the manor and noticed an elderly lady sitting at a small table. A sign behind her read "Entre 5." When Mr. S. asked, "Five what?" the lady replied, "What have you got?"

Mr. S., somewhat bewildered, responded, "I don't understand."

"What do you have in your wallet? Pounds, dollars, francs, or euros, whatever you have, the entrance fee is five of them."

"But that doesn't make any sense. The value of each of those currencies is so different."

"Maybe to those who travel high, wide, and handsome but not to local folks. Besides, it keeps the bookkeeping simple, and I don't have to worry about exchange rates. Do you wish to go in?"

"Sure, but I've only got pounds."

"Then that will be ten pounds."

Realizing that ten pounds was many times the value of, say, ten francs, Mr. S. was about to utter a complaint but saw the stern look in the old lady's eyes and chose to remain silent.

The woman gave him two tickets and said to give them to the butler, Basel, when they went through the front door. They crossed the front courtyard and, seeing the front door was open, walked in somewhat uneasily. At the foot of an old, long, curving, and stately stairway stood a wooden dummy dressed like a butler with a long-tailed tuxedo and white gloved hands, one of which was extended as if to receive the tickets.

"This is absurd. What do I do with these tickets?" said Mr. S.

"Why not just give the tickets to Basel as the lady requested?" suggested Bradley.

"Oh, very well."

After placing the tickets in the dummy's hand, the two walked into the grand entrance of the manor.

"Thank you."

"Did you hear that, Mr. S.?"

"Yes, it sounded like the dummy spoke to us. Hmmm, I suppose it was just our ears playing tricks on us."

"Yes, maybe."

As they walked into the grand drawing room, Bradley said out load, "My name is Bradley Flanagan and I've come from Kumquat Island to speak to the ghost of Gaston Y Goatwich. I would like to ask you to remove the spell from my friends, the McGuintys."

"Look out!" yelled Mr. S. as he pushed Bradley out of the way of a large statue that came crashing down right where he was standing.

"That was close," said Bradley as he stood up.

"Yes, we'd better go upstairs and see how that statue came loose," said Mr. S. As they made their way up the stairs, they could hear the faint sound of old-fashioned music from the 1940s.

"What's that music? Where's it coming from?" Bradley wondered aloud.

"I don't know, but it sounds like it's coming from upstairs."

When they reached the top landing, they walked down the hall towards the music. As they entered the room from where the music was coming, they saw an old-fashioned record player. Mr. S. walked over and turned it off.

"Someone must have left it on," said Mr. S.

"Maybe, but it wasn't on when we first came in," replied Bradley.

"Yes, you're right. Very interesting."

"Mr. S., look at these pictures on the wall."

"Why, these are pictures of German soldiers and what looks like the German countryside."

"Why would that be?"

"Well, these islands were occupied by the Nazis during the war. This was probably used as a headquarters by the officers," replied Mr. S.

The two continued to explore each of the rooms and noticed more pictures and memorabilia, including a German flag with a swastika on it. After going through all the rooms, the two returned to the long stairway. Just as Mr. S. started to walk down the long, steep stairs, he tripped and fell head over heels down the treacherous stairway. But as soon as Mr. S. started to tumble, he rolled himself into a tight ball and seemed to roll all the way down the stairs as if he were a soccer ball. Bradley ran down after him yelling, "Mr. S., are you all right?" He expected him to be very badly injured or worse.

Mr. S. stood up and brushed the dust off his sleeves and pants and said, "Yes, Bradley, I'm quite all right. But I want to see what caused me to trip at the top of the stairs." They climbed back up the stairs and were surprised to see a long nail sticking out of the top stair.

"That wasn't there when we first came up these stairs. That needs an explanation. And that statue falling down on you, that needs an explanation. I think it's clear that this ghost doesn't want to see you or me in this house. I'm going to take you back to The Watering Hole Pub to check if your Commander Didlittle has arrived yet and see if he can explain this."

CHAPTER 29
Commander Didlittle is Waiting

As Bradley and Mr. S. walked into the pub, Bradley could hear Commander Didlittle, in a loud but intimate whisper, addressing a number of patrons, who were leaning forward in their chairs and hanging on his every word.

"The cobra and I were just inches apart, staring at each other eyeball to eyeball, and just as the cobra was about to strike, my trusty and trained falcon swooped down, snatched him by the neck, and flew off with him into the blue sky!"

"Hi there, Commander Didlittle. I sure am glad to see you," said Bradley.

Didlittle turned and exclaimed, "Bradley, it's so good to see you, too!"

After Bradley introduced Commander Didlittle to Mr. S., Didlittle said, "I'll bet you boys are hungry."

"We sure are!" replied Bradley, suddenly remembering he hadn't eaten since that morning.

As the three were in the middle of their lunch, Mr. S.'s cell phone rang. He excused himself to take the call outside. A few minutes later, he came back in and explained that there had been an accident at one of his job-sites back in England and he would have to leave on the next ferry to the UK.

After seeing Mr. S. off at the ferry, Didlittle said to Bradley, "Now, Bradley, please tell me what you found on Guernsey Island."

After hearing Bradley's account of their scary visit to the haunted manor, Didlittle said, "Well, I can't say that I'm surprised. I'd always suspected that Gaston Y Goatwich was not going to be friendly."

"You mean he won't want to co-operate with us?"

"That's right."

"Then we're finished."

"Not necessarily."

"Why not?"

"Canterbury said that ghosts on the Channel Islands are usually pretty complex characters."

"Why is that?"

"I don't know exactly, but I remember he said these ghosts are usually free spirits and that can be good or bad."

"Oh yes, I remember you saying that before we left Kumquat Island."

"Right, now, hopefully, I'll be able to muster up Canterbury and get his advice on how to proceed."

CHAPTER 30
Calling Canterbury

"How will you get in touch with Canterbury?" asked Bradley.

"That should be easy. I'll simply recite the ancient rhyme."

> "Hammer and Sickle,
> I am deep in a pickle,
> But I need not worry,
> As I'll just call for Canterbury.
> Hicklesicklepickleticklemetoo."

"Okay, okay, what's cooking now, Diddy?"

"Canterbury, young Bradley here tried to make contact with Gaston Y Goatwich in his manor but without any success. In fact, Gaston tried to crush him with a falling statue. You realize we are running out of time to get the spell removed from the McGuintys before Bradley and his family are struck by the same spell. We urgently need some high-powered ghostal intervention! What are we to do?"

"Now, now, don't get a tangle in your bibby, Diddy. We haven't even put our best resource into play yet."

"And what is that, pray tell?"

"He's a ghost from another part of the island. The ghost of Dragonfly par la Mer."

"What has that ghost got to do with Gaston Y Goatwich?"

"Maybe a little, maybe a lot. We're going to find out soon enough."

"Please explain why we are going to spend what little time we have left talking to an unrelated ghost?"

"You don't know he is unrelated."

"Well then, please explain why we are going to see him."

"Oh, Didlittle, please be quiet for a moment, and I'll try to explain. While you were busy getting all mixed up at the ferry terminal and making time-wasting, unnecessary side trips, I was conducting some ghostal research. What I found was very interesting. You see, when the Nazis built the underground hospital during the war, they extended it out to the Gaston Y Goatwich manor."

"But why would they do that when they could have simply driven out to the manor?"

"Good question. Apparently, the Nazis were secretly using the manor as a spotting station to direct the V2 rockets they were sending into London in the last days of the war. Although it was to be a top secret Nazi project, the local people knew that the Gaston Y Goatwich manor was being used by the Nazis for something important."

"How did they know that?" inquired Didlittle.

"Because they noticed the large number of motorcycle dispatch riders that visited the manor. During the war, that was a sure sign that the place was being used for something important. That's why Gaston Y Goatwich's family was shunned during the war; they were seen to be collaborators. My ghostal research could only take me this far. If we want to find out more, then we have to visit Dragonfly par la Mer. Apparently he can tell us about a twist to this story that is not widely known."

"Well, what are we waiting for? Let's go see Dragonfly par la Mer and find out the rest of the story," said Didlittle enthusiastically.

CHAPTER 31
Visiting Dragonfly par la Mer

The manor of Dragonfly par la Mer stood majestically high on a protruding bluff that extended out to the sea. The front of the manor faced the famous Hanois lighthouse, which is on the westernmost point of the Channel Islands. Its fog horn and light have saved many ships from the perils of the jagged rock outcroppings that lie just below the surface on a high tide.

The families that resided in the manor throughout the nineteenth and twentieth centuries were always held in high regard by all the residents of the Channel Islands for their acts of courage to save sailors who were caught by angry seas off the rocks of Hanois lighthouse.

As Commander Didlittle, Bradley, and Canterbury entered the grounds of the now-abandoned manor, they couldn't help but notice a large well-manicured lawn surrounded by beautiful flowering shrubs and bushes.

Canterbury said, "Didlittle, I have a good feeling about this place. It has a nice aura about it."

"Yes, indeed, and the air is so clear, there's not an insect in sight. Why is that?" wondered Didlittle.

"Oh, Didlittle, you are a clever chap, you are. This estate is clear of all insects because of its namesake," replied Canterbury.

"I don't understand," said Bradley.

"This is the manor of Dragonfly par la Mer, which means 'Dragonfly by the sea' in English. The dragonflies you see with their pretty colours are desirable not only for their beauty, but also because they keep the premises clear of any flying insects."

"And these dragonflies look just like helicopters. Cool!" exclaimed Bradley. "It's a very nice place. Why is it abandoned?"

"Bradley, you are a very observant fellow. This manor's state of abandonment is the result of a very dramatic episode that occurred here many years ago, but more about that later. Let's see if we can find the ghostal host of the manor. Let's take a look around the back of the manor."

The three walked around to the back of the manor and across another expansive, beautiful lawn, where they saw a wispy ghost-like image of a tall man sitting at a garden table, staring out at the sea as it crashed over the jagged rocks protruding from it. Even sitting, he gave a haughty impression, with his long white hair being swirled about by the fresh wind off the sea.

CHAPTER 32
Breakfast with Dragonfly par la Mer

As the three approached the stately-looking gentleman, they noticed a dragonfly sitting on his shoulder.

"Good Morning, mes amis. I've been expecting you. I am the Earl of the manor and this is my trusted friend, Danforth. To you, he may just be a dragonfly but to me, he is my trustworthy companion. Welcome to the manor of Dragonfly par la Mer.

"Thank you. I am Commander Didlittle, this is Bradley, and this is..."

"And this is Canterbury. I know who you all are. I understand that you've been checking on me, Canterbury. What, pray tell, have you found out?"

"Good morning, Dragonfly par la Mer. Thank you for seeing us. I actually found out a lot about your gallant deeds, but would you be so kind as to tell your fascinating story to my friends here so that they can hear it first hand?"

"D'accord, but first, please sit down and join me in some breakfast."

The three sat down, but as they settled in, they noticed there was nothing on the table.

"Would you gentlemen care for some cream in your coffee? It's fresh from the dairy."

Canterbury, realizing they were having an imaginary meal, which is common fare for ghosts, responded quite calmly, "Yes, thank you. That would be nice."

"What about you, Bradley? Would you like some fresh orange juice to start?"

Bradley, seeing that they were playing a pretend breakfast, just like he played with his sister and mother back home, replied, "Yes, please. That would really hit the spot."

"What's going on here? I can't see any breakfast," said Didlittle in an unsettled tone.

Bradley, seeing that this was an awkward situation that could only get worse, jumped out of his chair and ran around to Didlittle and said, "Oh, Commander Didlittle, you are such a funny guy. These French breakfasts of coffee, orange juice, and fresh croissants are not as big and filling as the English breakfasts of sausages and eggs and such but they are so light and tasty." As Bradley said this, he stared directly into Didlittle's eyes and tried very hard to wink.

"What's wrong with your eye, young man? It looks like you've got something in it."

The commotion that surrounded looking at Bradley's eye took the attention off the imaginary breakfast and Canterbury said, "So, how about it, Dragonfly par la Mer? Would you be so kind as to share your story with my friends?"

"Yes, of course. I'd be happy to do that."

Chapter 33
"It was a stormy night..."

Dragonfly par la Mer leaned back in his chair and stared out at the rocks off the shore of the lighthouse as they were pounded by the rolling waves of the Atlantic Ocean. As he sat there quietly, he was mustering up all the memories of long ago. He then let out a long sigh, took a deep breath, and said, "The story that I'm going to tell you started on a stormy night in 1944. Just as the household was retiring to bed, there was a loud knock on the door. When I opened it, I saw the lighthouse keeper standing there in a high degree of agitation. I ushered him into the house and asked what brought him out on such a stormy night. He said that he was up at the top of the lighthouse after changing a bulb, and he was looking out to the west with binoculars when he saw a B17 crash into the sea. He said there was no explosion and he thought he saw some of the airmen get into dinghies just before the airplane sank. He and I rushed to the boathouse and launched the lifeboat. Two hours later, we had the five surviving crewmen safely hidden in our wine cellar. They had numerous injuries from the crash but were mended well enough to travel after two weeks. Now came the difficult part."

"First of all, you need to know that the Nazis had posted warnings that anyone providing shelter to Allied personnel would be shot in the city square. Second of all, the Earl of Gaston Y Goatwich was the only person on the island who had access to a motorized boat and the needed fuel to get back to England. Now, as you've probably heard, the Gaston Y Goatwich manor was secretly being used as a spotter station for the V2 rocket attacks on London. The entire island knew this and they shunned anyone who resided in the manor because they were thought to be collaborating with the Nazis."

"I had attended Cambridge with Gaston Y Goatwich, and we rowed together in 1938 when we beat Oxford, so we were pretty good friends. That's why I didn't go along with the notion that Gaston Y Goatwich was willingly collaborating with the Nazis."

"To make a long story longer, let me just say that I managed to make contact with Gaston Y Goatwich and asked for his help. Although reluctant at first, at great personal risk to him and his family, he provided a boat for the crewmen to escape back to England to fight another day. Naturally, because this was such a forbidden act, we all kept this a secret so no one on the island knew about this but the lighthouse keeper and my family. When the war was over, an islander reported the family of Gaston Y Goatwich to be Nazi collaborators and they were put on trail. My family and I stepped forward and testified that the Nazis used the Gaston Y Goatwich manor as the spotting station but the family had no choice in the matter. They were, in fact, prisoners in their own home."

"Just like us, back on Kumquat Island!" exclaimed Bradley.

"What was that?" asked Dragonfly par la Mer. Bradley proceeded to explain how he and his family were being held hostage by the McGuintys back home.

"That is very interesting and obviously why you are here, but we'll get to that in a moment," said Dragonfly par la Mer.

He then took a deep breath and continued his story. "In our testimony to the court, we provided a detailed account of how Gaston Y Goatwich had helped us get the crewmen safely away to England at great risk to himself and his family. Now you have to understand that the islanders were forced to live under very harsh conditions imposed by the Nazis and the hatred for anyone who was even suspected of helping them was very intense. The trail went on for a couple of weeks and the courthouse filled every day with people who'd suffered at the hands of the Nazis. Many had lost loved ones and they wanted revenge. They were convinced that the Gaston Y Goatwich family were guilty. Fortunately, the judge believed our testimony and the family was acquitted. Unfortunately, the community thought that we gave excessive credit to the Gaston Y Goatwich family to keep them from going to jail; they never forgave them."

"Eventually, they all moved away except for the Earl, who lived on for many years in the manor. He never invited anyone into the manor and never showed his face in the community until the day he died a bitter man. He continues to live there in spirit, and he is the one who placed the spell on the McGuinty family."

"Excuse me, if no real people live here anymore, how come the lawn and gardens are in such beautiful condition?" asked Bradley.

"Oh, Bradley, don't interrupt while Dragonfly par la Mer is telling his story," said Didlittle.

"No, no, that's quite all right. I'm finished. And besides, Bradley's observation is quite relevant to my story. You see, my family were fortunate to be the residents of this lovely manor for more than a century. Nearly two centuries, actually. And over all those years, we've been able to save the lives of many islanders whenever their sailboats or fish boats got driven onto those rocks out there. After the last of the Dragonfly par la Mer family had passed on, and that was me, the manor remained empty, the grounds began to wither away, and the weeds started to take over the garden. Then the local townspeople, only a couple at first, started to come out and tend the garden. Over time, the number of people working on the garden grew so that most of the island has a small hand in keeping the grounds in immaculate condition. I don't understand it really, but the people say they do it in appreciation for all the islander lives our family saved over the years."

"That is a terrific story. A story of courage and valour and a story worthy of the highest MOOGOO medal of merit. Absolutely terrific. I will report it to General Higginbottom. He's very high up in MOOGOO. I'm going to ask him to have you awarded with a medal," exclaimed Didlittle.

"Oh, Diddy, you just don't get it. My colleague Dragonfly par la Mer and I are of the spirit world. We have no use for physical tokens like medals," said Canterbury.

Dragonfly par la Mer paused and then continued, "Now, getting back to the issue of Gaston Y Goatwich. The only possible way of getting his attention is to make your approach through the Nazi underground tunnel that runs from the hospital to his manor."

"Why through there?" asked Didlittle.

"Because that's where he resides."

"But why don't we just go through the front door like Bradley did?"

"Because anyone going through the front is almost certainly a tourist, an islander, or a relative. Scaring the bejeezus out of them is Gaston's idea of revenge and his only source of amusement."

"Will just the fact that we're entering through the tunnel show that we're not merely looky-loo tourists?"

"Not necessarily. Over the years, there have been a couple of incidents where someone looking for a thrill has entered that way."

"What happened?"

"They've come running out of the tunnel scared to death. You see, Gaston considers the tunnel to be his private chambers, and he probably doesn't like to be disturbed. That's why he behaves so badly when someone enters the tunnel."

"Well, what about us? We'll be invading his privacy too," said Didlittle.

"True, and that's why you must persevere no matter how scary it gets."

"Persevere to do what, get a heart attack form sheer terror?" asked Didlittle with a mounting air of trepidation.

"Persevere until you can get him to reveal his likeness to you so that you can engage in conservation."

"How do we do that?"

"There's two parts to it."

"What do you mean, two parts?"

"Two parts: the first part is to get him to reveal his likeness to you."

"How do we do that?"

"You keep repeating Canterbury's ancient rhyme."

"Will he know that rhyme?"

"No, but it'll hopefully show him you're not just thrill-seeking islanders. And, if so, he'll appear before you."

"Once Gaston shows his likeness, will it then be clear sailing?"

"I don't know, maybe, but one can't be sure. You see, Gaston has had a tough go of it with his running vendetta with the islanders. He's a little unpredictable."

"Oh, an unhappy, unpredictable ghost. That sounds scary!" exclaimed Bradley.

"Not to worry, Bradley. I didn't get to where I am today without being able to handle the unpredictable. In fact, it can be said, no, it actually has been said that I am a specialist in the unpredictable. In fact, you could call me Mr. Unpredictable!"

"That's for sure," said Canterbury quietly under his breath.

"Like I was saying," continued Dragonfly par la Mer, "if he appears before you, that will indicate he may be willing to talk, but it's no guarantee."

"So how will we get him to talk to us?"

"I'm going to give you a secret code that will tell him you were sent by me and only me."

"How will he know that?"

"Because I'm giving you the name of the skull we rowed in for Cambridge. He and I are the only ones who know that name."

"And what is that?"

"Twenty-three Skidoo."

"Twenty-three Skidoo? That's an unusual name for a boat."

"Indeed it is. That's why Gaston will be sure you were sent by me. Tell him your story and say that I gave you the code to verify that your story is true."

"Okey Dokey, Twenty-three Skidoo it is then. Now, if you can issue us the directional co-ordinates of our path to the covert tunnel entrance, we can take that intelligence and convert it into a straightforward military plan of attack," said Didlittle.

"What did he say?" asked Dragonfly par la Mer, turning to Canterbury.

"He wants to know how to get to the tunnel," replied Canterbury.

"Okay, now pay attention because this is a little tricky. Once you enter the hospital, take the elevator down to the bottom floor, the Blue floor. Then turn right and proceed down the main hall following the blue line. At the second cross hall, turn left and follow the yellow line, which turns right and becomes the purple line at the next cross hall. Follow that purple line to the next cross hall and then turn right. A short distance along that hall, you'll see an orange door and a green door. Now this is very important. You are to go through the orange door and not, I repeat not, through the green door. This is very important that you get this clear. You go through the orange door and not the green door. Is that clear?"

"Más claro que agua," said Didlittle.

"What was that?" asked Dragonfly par la Mer.

"Más claro que agua, more clear than water. It's a Spanish expression I picked up when I was on an undercover mission in the Basque hills of Spain."

Bradley, concerned about the directions, asked, "What if we go through the green door instead of the orange door?"

"Then your mission may be doomed to failure," replied Dragonfly par la Mer.

"Why?" asked Bradley.

"Because the green door is an old emergency escape chute installed by the Nazis. That chute goes all the way down to the sea on the far side of the island. I think it goes directly into the sea so that the escaping Nazis could be picked up by a waiting U-boat. But I'm not sure about that. One thing's for sure, if you fall down that chute, you'll be in a lot of trouble. So remember it's the orange door, not the green door."

"No problem. We'll just treat this mission like a colour-coded military mission. It's blue, yellow, purple, green, orange. Have I got those colours right?"

"Ah, yes," replied Dragonfly par la Mer a little hesitantly.

"Well, that's it then, isn't it? No need to muck about. It's time to get the lead out, put some wind in our sails, and get this show on the road. I didn't get to where I am today by laying about when there was a task to be done…"

"Oh put a cork in it, Diddy!" said Canterbury. "Dragonfly par la Mer, thank you for your help. If you're ever in Canterbury hamlet and I can be of assistance, please call me. With your permission, we will now take our leave."

"Au revoir, mes amis, et bon chance."

CHAPTER 34
Which Door?

The next morning, after getting directions to the hospital, which was on the edge of town, Didlittle walked briskly towards its entrance, located at the end of a long old cobbled street with high stone walls on each side. As they approached the hospital, they could see that it was built of concrete in a military bunker-like style. Although its structure was much bigger and very different from the surrounding old stone buildings, it seemed to blend in since its surface had been etched, pitted, and stained by the relentless ocean winds blowing sand and stone over the years.

"How will we be able to get down to the tunnel entrance without being stopped by security, Commander Didlittle?" asked Bradley.

"No problem, young man. It's merely a case of strutting in with determination to give the impression that one knows exactly where one is going. The whole world stands aside for the man who knows where he is going. Now just strut like I do and keep your chin up high."

"Yes, sir!" exclaimed Bradley, and he strutted like Didlittle to get into the mood of their act as they approached the hospital entrance.

Opening the front door with gusto, they walked towards the front desk. Didlittle announced in a loud voice, "Commander Didlittle is the name, and military intelligence is my game. My colleague, Bradley Flanagan, and I have very important business to attend to here today."

The nurses were deep in a discussion about shift scheduling and paid them no attention as they walked past them to the elevators. Once in the elevator, Didlittle started to chant, "Blue, Yellow,

Purple, Green, Orange; it's the orange, not the green, not the green but the orange; it's the orange, not the green," over and over so that by the time the elevator reached their floor, even Bradley was getting confused about the doors.

After navigating the colour-coded hallways, Didlittle briskly marched up to the two doors, swung one open, and stepped in before Bradley could stop him.

"Oh, noooooooo. It's the other door, Bradley!" cried Didlittle as he disappeared down the chute.

CHAPTER 35
The Haunted Tunnel

Bradley was dumbfounded. What was he to do? Should he follow Didlittle down the chute to see if he needed help? Or should he go in the orange door and enter the tunnel by himself to see if he could make contact with Gaston Y Goatwich? Or should he just go back to the front desk and report that Commander Didlittle had an accident and he needed help. This was a very difficult decision. His dad had always told him that when faced with a tough decision, he should add up the pros and cons of each one and then choose.

Going after Didlittle would put them both on the wrong side of the island and Dragonfly par la Mer said that could likely doom the success of their mission. He knew that Didlittle wouldn't want that. If he reported to the front desk that Didlittle went through the green door, it would certainly lead them to evicting him from the hospital, if not taking him into custody. That would certainly mean there would be no chance of getting back to the orange door, and their mission would be a failure. After considering these alternatives, Bradley realized that his only choice was to go through the orange door by himself, even though the thought scared the dickens out of him.

So, Bradley drew in a long breath, turned the knob on the orange door, and stepped in. The tunnel was totally black when the orange door slammed behind him. Bradley stood still for a few minutes until his eyes became accustomed to the dark. He looked around and saw a large tunnel leading away from the orange door. As he started to walk slowly down the tunnel, he looked up and saw cobwebbed timbers on the ceiling with sleeping bats hanging from them. Bradley was glad they were sleeping, but he couldn't help but wonder what happened when they all woke up and started flying around the tunnel. As Bradley walked farther down the tunnel, he felt a breeze come up that blew directly into his face. As each minute passed, the breeze grew stiffer and then it became a full wind that made a howling sound. Small rocks and pebbles blown by the wind started to hit Bradley in the face, which he tried to protect with his hands. By now the wind had climbed to the intensity of a full force 8 gale, with lots of debris smashing into Bradley. Struggling to move ahead, Bradley finally had to stop his progress and move against the tunnel wall to try to avoid the full force of the wind and all the debris that was hitting and bruising him.

Once Bradley got himself settled in a leaning position against the tunnel wall, he stared out at the missiles flying by in the wind and suddenly realized that they were bats, thousands of them. That explained the eerie squealing sound reverberating throughout the tunnel. It was then that Bradley realized his bruises were inflicted by the flying bats.

Bradley wasn't sure why the bats weren't running into him now. Maybe, he thought, it was because he was out of the main-stream of the tunnel and he was standing still, which enabled the bats' radar to more easily identify his presence. But did that mean he'd have to stand there for a long time waiting for the bats to stop flying? And how could he be sure that the bats wouldn't eventually attack him?

Bradley decided he would much prefer to be at home with his mom and dad and not in this bat-infested tunnel and turned to head back to the orange door. But before he took a step in retreat, he stopped and thought of his grandfather Freddy Flanagan, who was a highly-decorated soldier in World War II.

Whenever he felt frightened, his grandfather used to quote General Paton: "Courage is fear holding on one more minute." So for Grandpa's sake, Bradley chose to stay on one more minute and started to count to sixty. When he got to sixty, he chose to count to sixty again. And when he got to sixty, he started again. He lost

count of how many times he counted to sixty, but it was quite a few. Then without any warning, the wind and the bats just disappeared and the tunnel became very still and quiet.

"AHHHOOOOO, AHHHOOOO. How dare you invade my privacy. Other triflers who've entered this tunnel ran back when I turned the bats loose on them. Why do you persist with staying in this tunnel? Can't you see that it's haunted and you're not welcome?"

Bradley was extremely frightened by now and wasn't sure what to say. However, he remembered his mom saying that if you're not sure what to say, then starting out with good manners is a good step forward. "Excuse me, Mr. Ghost. I mean no disrespect, sir, but I am supposed to recite to you the ancient rhyme of Canterbury," said Bradley, and he proceeded to repeat the Canterbury rhyme over and over again.

"What is that rhyme about anyway?" said a voice from within the tunnel.

"It's the ancient rhyme for the ghost of Canterbury. It's to show you that I believe in and understand ghosts," said Bradley.

"You do, do you? Why should I believe you?"

"Twenty-three Skidoo."

"What was that?"

"Twenty-three Skidoo."

"Where did you get that phrase from?"

"From the ghost of Dragonfly par la Mer. He said that it was the name of the skull you two rowed when you were at Cambridge together."

"And why did he give it to you?"

"He said that when we got to talk to you, to tell you that he was using Twenty-three Skidoo as a code to assure you that we have credibility. He said to ask you to listen to our story as a favour to him," said Bradley.

"Hmm, interesting. I owe a lot to Dragonfly par la Mer and his family. They were about the only ones on the island that stood by us. Your credentials are sound. Now, you keep saying 'we.' Is there someone else with you?"

"Yes, sir, Commander Didlittle."

"Commander Didlittle, who's he?"

"Oh, he's the brilliant Commander of the very famous Lost Battalion, sir."

"And where is he?"

"Ah, well, sir, you see, sir, well, he went through the green door and fell down the chute. But he's the Commander in charge of this mission, and I'm just his helper."

"He can't be much of a Commander if he couldn't find the right door to the tunnel."

"But, with respect, sir, it's quite confusing having the two doors so close together and especially after following all those coloured lines."

"But you managed to go through the right door. Well, never mind about your Commander Didlittle. You got here to deliver your message. What is your name, young man?"

"Bradley Flanagan, sir."

Suddenly a wispy grey-haired ghostlike image appeared. Bradley jumped back in fright, and then after a moment, Bradley noticed there was something about this ghost that was similar to Dragonfly par la Mer. They both had long, lean figures. Then Bradley remembered they had rowed together at Cambridge. They were both long and lean just like rowers would be.

"I'm glad to meet you, Bradley. You've shown remarkable courage to stand up to my scary bat haunt in this tunnel. So tell me your story."

CHAPTER 36
What's behind the Green Door?

Commander Didlittle slid down the chute as fast as greased lightning. Judging by the speed of the wind blowing through his hair, Didlittle estimated he was reaching speeds of 60 miles per hour!

The chute had a number of turns and curves in it, and it reminded Didlittle of when he went on a "shoot the chute" ride as a young child with his father one summer at the Brighton amusement dock south of London. In fact, Didlittle was just starting to enjoy the ride down the chute when he was propelled out of the chute and onto a gigantic mattress. Didlittle had the wind knocked out him momentarily from the sudden stop on the mattress.

Shaken but not hurt, he climbed off the mattress onto an underground dock. Didlittle hesitated a moment to get used to the dim light and then started to observe his surroundings. He was on a dock in a deep underground waterway that had a U-boat moored to it.

He squinted his eyes to get a better focus in the poor light. As his eyes became adjusted to the light, he saw a large cigar-light vessel with a gun turret mounted on the front deck, and at midships, there was a conning tower with a faded call letter U-571. Didlittle was astonished when he realized he was looking at a German submarine from World War II.

"Achtung! Sprechen sie Deutsch?" someone said in German.

Realizing that the sound came from behind him, Didlittle slowly turned around and was utterly spellbound by the sight he beheld. A half dozen German sailors were standing in a line behind an officer who was pointing a Luger at him. The situation, with an old enemy officer pointing a pistol at him, might have been unnerving if it weren't for the condition of the whole bunch. The officer and the soldiers were very, very old and feeble-looking. It looked like they hadn't shaved for several years, as they all had long grey beards. They all had bloodshot eyes from many years in the dark and their uniforms were torn and moth-eaten.

"Nein, Ich spreche nur Englisch," replied Didlittle in perfect German.

"Oh, well then, before we put you in irons and lock you up, tell us how the war is going."

"What war?" asked Didlittle.

"The war that's going on right now, of course."

"Well, Hymie, I've got some bad news for you. You lost the war."

"We did? When did that happen, and when are they coming to pick us up?"

"The war ended in 1945, which was fifty years ago, and no one is coming to pick you up."

"I can't believe it's been that long, but it's hard to tell without a calendar. Mind you, our supplies are getting low. In fact, we ran out of razor blades two years ago."

"Yes, I noticed," said Didlittle.

"What is your name, British soldier?"

"Didlittle is the name, and military intelligence is the game. You see, I am much more than a mere British soldier. I am Commander Didlittle, Commander of the famous Lost Battalion."

"Where is your famous battalion?"

"Ah, well, they are being held captive in a stockade on Kumquat Island."

"Where's Kumquat Island, and why are they being held captive there?"

"Well, that's a long story. Let me start..."

"Don't start any long stories. At our ages, we don't have time for long stories, but I have a question for you."

"What's that?"

"Do you have a first-aid kit on you?"

"Of course I have a first-aid kit. I didn't get to be where I am today by not having my trusty first-aid kit with me at all times," replied Didlittle.

"Good, then I'll make a deal with you. You let me have a couple of aspirins for my splitting headache, and I'll give you my Lugar."

"That's a deal."

CHAPTER 37
Didlittle Captures Headlines and Germans

A few hours later, a call went out from the nearby lighthouse, "This is the lighthouse keeper at St Samson, Harry Cripps, calling for the harbourmaster at St. Peter Port, over."

"This is the harbourmaster of St. Peter Port, Johny Jenkins. Go ahead, Harry."

"Johny, you're not going to believe this. Do you remember hearing about the German U-boat U-571 stationed here during the war that was never found?"

"Yes, I remember hearing about it. My dad helped the British Marines search for it for months, but they couldn't find any sign of it."

"Well, you're not going to believe your eyes. If you train your binoculars in a north-easterly direction, you'll see a very unusual sight entering your harbour. Take a look and confirm you've got a sighting."

Johny picked up his binoculars and aimed them out in the direction Harry suggested.

"Oh, my goodness. I don't believe it!" Johny exclaimed.

"What do you see?"

"I see the German U-boat clearly marked U-571 with a British officer at the helm in the conning tower."

"Isn't that unbelievable?"

"Yes, but there's more."

"What's that?"

"There's a big banner hanging from the tower."

"What does it say?"

"It says 'MOOGOO' on one side and 'This U-boat has been captured single-handedly by Commander Didlittle' on the other side."

"Who's Commander Didlittle?"

"I don't know, but I've a feeling we're all going to find out! I can see some newspaper men and TV broadcasters gathering on the dock to greet him as we speak."

CHAPTER 38
Bradley Can Say Mission Accomplished

Gaston Y Goatwich told Bradley to take his time and to tell him all the details of his story. So it was nearly two hours before Bradley finished telling everything that happened on Kumquat Island over the past three months. When Bradley was finished, Gaston said, "So Stinkworthy isn't the rightful owner of the Kumquat Island Coffee Company?"

"Absolutely not!"

"And the McGuintys and Flanagans aren't trying to steal the company away from him? And, in fact, they are the rightful owners?"

"You are absolutely correct, sir."

"And Stinkworthy is an undercover agent for the Daddybeans Coffee Company that is trying to take away the company from your family and the McGuintys?"

"Yes, sir."

"It looks like this Stinkworthy has played me for a fool, and he's caused a lot of hardship for your family and the McGuintys, especially the McGuintys."

"That's also correct, sir."

"Well, then, we'll just have to get this situation corrected, won't we."

"How will we do that, sir?"

"Hmmmm, that's a good question, Bradley. Let's see..." said Gaston Y Goatwich as he stared out into space. "Yes, I've got it. Ask Commander Didlittle to order Stinkworthy up to your home after you've returned and celebrated with the McGuintys."

"Celebrated? What will we celebrate?" asked Bradley with a mounting level of curiosity and excitement.

"Oh, you'll find out in good time, my brave young chap."

Bradley wasn't sure, but he thought he saw a gleam in Gaston Y Goatwich's eye...that is if a ghost can have a gleam in its eye.

CHAPTER 39
Didlittle Prevails Once More

The next day, Bradley couldn't believe his good fortune in meeting up with Commander Didlittle. Here he was riding in a fancy horse-drawn carriage with Didlittle in a parade arranged to honour him for his capture of the famous missing U-boat, U-571, and the remaining German sailors (who by this time were being treated at the local old-folks home).

The parade started at dockside in the harbour of St. Peter Port, where the now-famous U-boat was moored, and it wandered all the way through downtown to the city hall, where they were greeted by the mayor and a jubilant crowd of cheering citizens from Guernsey Island.

The mayor made a few remarks about how grateful all the citizens were to Commander Didlittle for finding and apprehending the missing U-boat. The mayor then asked Didlittle if he'd like to make a speech.

Didlittle stepped up to the microphone and said that he didn't like to make speeches. He said that he didn't get to where he was today by making speeches; no, that was not for him. He said he got to be Commander by being a man of action and a man of very few words. Speeches were something he avoided, he claimed. And he went on to say that there was nothing more boring that listening to somebody giving a speech who had nothing to say. Didlittle went on to talk about MOOGOO, Hawksbury, the Lost Battalion, and all the regions he'd served in. He then went on to talk about how qualified he was to be a Commander by citing all the schools he'd attended and all the night-school courses he'd enrolled in (even though he'd never finished any of them).

After listening to Didlittle speak for over an hour, most of the crowd had drifted away and gone about their shopping and downtown chores. Didlittle concluded by saying, "As I've said before, I didn't get to be where I am today without the unique ability to always do the unpredictable. In fact, you could call me Mr. Unpredictable. But, I prefer you call me Commander Didlittle, since that is my true name and calling. Are there any questions?"

By now, the crowd had shrunk to just a remaining few, who were either reading newspapers or doing crosswords puzzles. Didlittle then said, "And so with those few remarks, Mr. Mayor, I wish to say thank you for recognizing my amazing achievement of capturing the last remaining U-boat of the German naval fleet."

As Didlittle turned towards the mayor, he saw that the mayor was fast asleep. Not missing a beat, Didlittle called out, "Tally ho, Bradley. We must now be off to the airport."

The movement on the stage roused the mayor, who jumped up and pretended to have been awake. He then led the two to a limousine and sent them off to the airport.

As they entered the airport, Bradley said, "Commander Didlittle, sir, can I ask you a question?"

"Of course, Bradley. What is it?"

"How are we going to fly home? There are no airline connections to Kumquat Island."

"The same way we got here, by ghostal transport," replied Didlittle.

Commander Didlittle led Bradley over to a deserted part of the air terminal and quietly recited the ancient rhyme, concluding with "Hicklesicklepickleticklemetoo."

A brief moment later, Canterbury appeared.

"So, how's the mission going now?" asked Canterbury as he appeared before their eyes.

"Jolly swell, just jolly swell. Bradley here has been a big help. We not only made contact with Gaston Y Goatwich, but I also managed to capture a missing U-boat and a squad of German sailors," replied Didlittle.

"Oh, Diddy, you are quite amazing. Very well, then let's get you two back to Kumquat Island."

CHAPTER 40
Stinkworthy's Surprise

Stinkworthy was getting anxious. He had not had a message on the cell phone for over three days. What was Daddybeans Coffee doing? Why hadn't they contacted him?

Leaning against the stockade fence, he took another sip of the morning coffee offered at mid-morning each day by the McGuintys. He had to admit, the coffee was exceptional, and he could see why Daddybeans Coffee Company wanted to get control of the Kumquat Island Coffee Company.

"Stinkworthy, we've been ordered back to the Flanagan home by Commander Didlittle on the double," announced Hawk as he rushed up to Stinkworthy with an air of urgency.

"When do we leave?" asked Stinkworthy with some enthusiasm.

"Right now. I've had Doggie dig out the escape hole for us, and he'll come along as our guide. He knows the island like the back of his hand."

After a long march at a brusque pace, the Flanagan home came into sight.

"What could have come up that has the Flanagans wanting me in a hurry?" wondered Stinkworthy as they approached the front door.

After a sharp knock, Matt Flanagan swung open the door and said, "Welcome, gentlemen. Come in, please."

As they walked into the front room, Stinkworthy glanced around the room and saw Commander Didlittle, Bradley, Maria, Monica, and Jason Flanagan. They were all standing, and Stinkworthy had an uneasy feeling that they were all staring at him.

"Hello, Stink. How are things down at Refuge Beach? Are the McGuintys being tough on you?" asked Didlittle.

"Ah no, actually the McGuintys have treated all of us in the camp pretty well."

"That's good. Now Stink, tell us, why did you come to this island anyway?"

"Why, I heard on the radio that there had been an uprising on the island, so I came to see how I could help."

"Oh, that's good, Stink, and do you think that you did?"

"Did what, sir?" asked Stinkworthy, who was starting to feel very uneasy about the line of questioning.

"Did you help?"

"Did I help what?"

"That's what we'd like to know."

"I'm sorry, sir, but I don't understand your line of questioning."

"Oh, never mind, Stink. I was just having some fun at your expense. We have a little surprise for you. Bradley, would you please ask the McGuinty family to join us now?"

Stinkworthy was dumbfounded to hear that the shrunken McGuintys were in the Flanagan home.

Bradley opened the back door and said, "Mr. McGuinty, would you please come in now."

Into the room walked Squinty McGuinty and all his family, who were now full-sized, and Tobius, at 6 feet 2 inches, loomed large to all who could see him.

The sight of Tobius brought tears to Monica and her mother. Monica yelled "Tobius!" and ran over to him, threw her arms about his neck, and gave him a big kiss. There was a long pause for all the Flanagans and McGuintys to savour the sweetness of the moment.

"Now, Stink, did you give any thought to how inconvenient severe shrinkage was on the McGuinty family?" asked Didlittle.

"I don't know what you mean, sir," said Stinkworthy with the sound of fear in his voice.

"Oh, come on now, Stink, think. Did you not realize that Commander Didlittle and the Lost Battalion would succeed on this mission just like they always do? Surely you knew that by applying strict military intelligence procedures, I would eventually expose your dastardly plot, which was a very nasty piece of business."

"I don't know what you mean," said Stinkworthy weakly.

"Oh, yes you do. Does Gaston Y Goatwich mean anything to you? It should. He was the one you lied to in order to get the shrinking spell placed on the McGuintys."

Stinkworthy, now realizing that the jig was up, thought about bolting for the door, but something very strange was happening to him. Everybody and everything was getting larger and larger. He was bewildered, but then he suddenly realized that he was shrinking. After a few minutes, Stinkworthy was down to six inches in height.

"How will we keep him in custody until the authorities arrive?" asked Matt.

"Your son, Bradley, already has that figured out. Bradley, please take Stink into custody and put him behind bars to await the arrival of the authorities."

With that order, Bradley scooped up Stinkworthy in his right hand and placed him into the prison cell of his Lincoln Log cabin set, which was the perfect size for anyone six inches tall.

CHAPTER 41
Bradley's Reward

"I now pronounce you man and wife," said the reverend flown in to preside over the marriage of Monica Flanagan and Tobius McGuinty.

It was a beautiful wedding ceremony in a little chapel that was overflowing with happy family and friends. The married couple exited the chapel and walked under the ceremonial trellis of the rifles of all six hundred men of the Lost Battalion, who served as the honour guard. Walking directly behind the handsome couple was Bradley, bursting with pride as he was the BEST MAN.

As the married couple stepped into the 4 wheel drive that would take them to the Kumquat Island Coffee Company private airport to fly off on their honeymoon, Commander Didlittle walked up to Squinty McGuinty and said, "All right then, it's Squinty McGuinty, Esquire, is it? Okay, then Squinty McGuinty, Esquire, how about if we find ourselves a pint of bitter, and I'll tell you about our Channel Island adventure?"

"You know, Didlittle, I might have grossly underestimated your abilities."

"Most people do, my friend. Most people do."

About the Authors

Callum Shepard is a grade 4 student. He has a variety of interests that range from swimming, skiing, and tennis to arts and computer games. Callum loves mythology and is an avid reader. He looks forward to touring the castles of Britain with his Grampa.

Macgregor Shepard is a grade 6 student. He loves rugby, basketball, swimming, and golf. He is an expert on military history, specializing in World War II. In 2009, he toured the beaches of Normandy with his Grampa.

James Shepard (Grampa), 70, spent many years with a Caterpillar dealership. On retirement, he wanted to do something creative. He found paragliding too scary and running marathons too tiresome. His two grandsons, Callum and Macgregor, inspired him to help them create the laughable, lovable, over-the-top Commander Didlittle character and his Lost Battalion, and his antics are, if nothing else, creative.

The Shepard family lives in Vancouver, BC, Canada.